Gunfight at
Dragoon Springs

Rancher Tom Bligh thinks his financial troubles are over when he sells his herd at Fort Yuma in Arizona. But on his way home to his ranch in the Dragoon mountains his gold is stolen in a stagecoach hold-up by the bandit known as El Mexicano. It is a case of get the money back or kiss goodbye to his ranch – and Bligh is not a man to take the loss of his money and his home lying down.

With Emilio Chavez, a border patrol officer from Mexico, he sets out to track down the thief. Then there's the beautiful gambler Frankie Lewis, who has more to do with the loss of his money than he had ever suspected.

In Bligh's life, the girl and the gold are just two of the complications.

Gunfight at Dragoon Springs

WALT MASTERSON

A Black Horse Western

ROBERT HALE · LONDON

© Walt Masterson 2008
First published in Great Britain 2008

ISBN 978-0-7090-8546-1

Robert Hale Limited
Clerkenwell House
Clerkenwell Green
London EC1R 0HT

www.halebooks.com

The right of Walt Masterson to be identified as
author of this work has been asserted by him
in accordance with the Copyright, Designs and
Patents Act 1988

Typeset by
Derek Doyle & Associates, Shaw Heath
Printed and bound in Great Britain by
Antony Rowe Limited, Wiltshire

For the three Bs – Brenda, Barrie and Bob – who keep the Northern watch.

CHAPTER ONE

It had been a long, hot haul up from Maricopa Wells and the horses were labouring and blowing hard when they came to the top of the incline and made the turn to take them down into the valley and towards Tucson far to the south.

Tom Bligh took his hat off and wiped the band with a bandanna already sweaty from the springtime heat, then rammed it back over his eyes. The sun was flooding into the big Concorde coach and straight into his face, and somebody had pulled the shade down so hard that he had pulled it off its hinges and left the offside passenger with no protection.

But there is no better practice for sleeping while on the move than herding 2000 head of cattle over rough, hot rocky territory, so to his own surprise, he slept. And, sleeping, lost all his money.

He was aware, through the fog of his sleep, that the stage pulled up suddenly, and heard through slowly awakening ears, voices shouting. But it was the shot, close by and startlingly loud, which really awakened him and by that time, it was too late.

As he sat upright, the woman who had been sitting

7

opposite him screamed like a steamboat whistle, and a voice bellowed, only feet away, for her to shut up.

Instinctively, he reached for his gun but a pistol muzzle was jammed into his face just under the cheekbone, and a man shouted, 'Move and you're dead, mister! Move and you are D-E-D!'

The spelling might not have been good, but the message was crystal clear, and he froze still as a dead polar bear in fifty below.

'You! Shut your mouth, girl, and take their guns, and throw them out of the window. Then fill this bag with money, and do it quick, or you ain't leaving here without a box!'

She gathered the guns and did as he said, then took the burlap sack and with trembling hands started to empty her reticule into it.

'Not that, you silly heifer – the money. Get their money, get their rings, get their stick-pins and their wallets. All or nothing! *Todo o nada*! Move!'

She was holding her hysteria down but her face was deathly white, and she went through their pockets with hands which trembled so much she twice dropped things she was trying to get in the bag. When she got to Bligh, she took his heavy money bag with an apologetic look, obviously startled at its weight. There was the price of a small ranch in that bag, in gold coin. His gold coin. His ranch.

Bligh took a chance to glance at the hold-up man, and was startled to see a face from a nightmare looking back at him. The man was wearing a white bag over his head with a grotesque parody of a face hacked into it.

The head was crowned with black, woolly 'hair', the eyes burned holes in the material. Where the nose should

8

be, a cone-shaped fold had been sewn into the material. There was a scarlet slash where the mouth would normally appear.

'Quick! Quick! You want to die here? Give me the bag, now!'

She handed it clumsily through the window and, as she did so, she leaned over Bligh's lap and he felt a weight drop on to his knee. He put his hand on it and found himself holding a pocket Colt revolver.

'Now, get back from the window, and sit down. Do it now!'

The robber wheeled his horse away from the coach window, and Bligh heard him fire twice. The coach rocked as the horses plunged and whinnied, and he stuck his head out of the window and cursed when he saw that the bandit had shot into the two lead horses. One of them was down, the other thrashing in its traces, one leg broken and blood spurting from the wound in its hip.

There was a clatter as the gunman came back towards the coach, his pistol extended and pointing at the driver on his seat. Caught half in and half out of the window, Bligh fired once, twice, and saw something fly from the shoulder of the bandit's coat. The man swore loudly and fired back, though wildly because his horse was plunging, and then he was away, his horse hammering for the downward slope of the hill.

Bligh dropped from the coach and threw one last shot after the disappearing figure, but the little pistol had no range, and where the ball went he could not tell. It did not seem to affect the fleeing road agent, so he assumed it was a clean miss.

He walked back to the coach and fired the final two

cartridges into the heads of the two wounded horses, and watched each in turn relax into death. Then he helped the driver calm the remaining four, unfastened the traces of the dead animals, and recovered them for the driver.

The young woman who had given him the gun had got down from the coach and was bandaging the wound of the guard, who seemed to be the only casualty. The man had taken a flesh wound in the shoulder, and was white with shock, for the big slug had quite an impact, but one of the other passengers produced a bottle of whiskey from his bag, and helped wash out the wound and poured some into the wounded man's throat as well.

The girl said, 'Did you hit him?'

He realized he was still holding her pistol, and emptied the spent shells before he gave it back to her.

'Thanks. I don't think he has finished with us, yet,' he said. 'My name's Tom Bligh.'

It seemed a very inadequate thing to say to a woman who had risked a great deal for them all, but the girl did not seem to take offence. She produced a box of shells from her handbag and reloaded the pistol as she talked. Her hands were neat and sure and he knew without asking that she was a good shot.

'I'm Frankie Lewis, Mr Bligh,' she said. 'It's a pity you missed him, because I think he will be back.'

'Why?' asked Tanner, the driver. She shrugged.

'It's a feeling I have,' she said. She had remarkable eyes, Bligh noticed. They were green like a stormy sea and had a level, steady look. A woman to be reckoned with, he thought. He wondered what she was doing out here, where women tended to be decorative and work in saloons, or careworn and work on their husbands'

10

ranches. Either way of life used up a woman fast, and western women tended to be tough, hard-working and looked it.

This girl, though, was a beauty who would not have been out of place in one of the great houses in the land.

She was tall, with dark hair and a smooth skin which had not suffered from the western weather. Unlike the fashionable beauties he had seen in San Francisco and Los Angeles, she was tanned, and looked as though the feel of the wind on her face was familiar to her. He wondered what such a woman was doing out here, and why he had not heard of her before. If she had been around for long, she would have been a subject of comment and speculation in every saloon in the territory.

The drummer from the west coast had come this far by rail, and he was shocked by the sudden and uncaring violence out on the open desert. He was, he explained, now taking his samples on to Tucson and later Tombstone. He was examining his empty wallet ruefully.

'Got all my cash,' he said sadly. 'Where's the nearest bank with a telegraph? I got to get more from head office.'

The driver gave a snort of laughter. 'Tucson or maybe Phoenix but you got to get there, mister. This here stage is going back to Maricopa Wells, or I'm liable to lose my shotgun man. I don't like the look of Japhet's shoulder, not one little bit.'

'Back? But I paid for a passage through to Tucson. I got to get there as soon as possible. I can't get any money back at Maricopa Wells.'

The driver shrugged. 'If he left you something you can hock, I guess Hermann back at Maricopa will advance you something, but it won't be a fortune. My shotgun man's

11

got a wife and four kids, and another on the way. They ain't got no money, and if Japhet cashes in his chips, they ain't got no breadwinner, neither.'

'But—'

'You can come back to Maricopa Wells with us, and I guess the company will honour your ticket for tomorrow. You already paid for meals on the road, so you won't starve.'

He helped Bligh put the guard into the coach and settled him in the corner. The man's face was grey with shock and loss of blood, and the ride back to Maricopa Wells was going to be agony for him. Bligh handed him the remains of the whiskey silently, and their eyes met with understanding. The wounded man nodded his thanks, and Bligh winked.

'Ride easy,' he said. 'And don't forget to loosen that tourniquet every couple of hours, or you'll lose that arm. I'll get the guns and ride shotgun back to Maricopa. Maybe they'll hire me to see the stage through to Tucson.'

He walked out into the desert and began to collect the firearms the bandit had made Frankie throw away. When he came back, he had four pistols in his hands, and the guard's Greener. It was a solid, short barrelled shotgun and when he broke it to check the load, it was filled with buckshot. He ejected the shells and checked them.

'If you'd got off one shot, you'd like to cut him in half,' Bligh opined, reloading both barrels. 'He take you by surprise?'

The driver shook out the traces and brought the coach round to point back to Maricopa Wells. He flicked the whip out and slowed the coach as it came past Bligh, who caught the rail with one hand and vaulted back on to the box. Bligh rested the shotgun across his knees and checked the load in his Colt.

The driver glanced at it sideways.

'One of them new Colt's Lightnings?' he asked, eyeing the curve of the butt. 'Seen one in Phoenix, but ain't come across anybody uses one yet.'

Bligh grinned tightly. 'Fine weapon. Double action, so you don't need to cock her every pop,' he said. 'Just point and pull and she does the rest.'

He whirled it round his finger and dropped the weapon back into his holster. He hooked the thong over the hammer spur to prevent the weapon from dropping out of the holster, and glanced at the driver.

'About as useful as a lump of rock, if you can't get your hand on her at the right time,' he added bitterly. 'Single or double, you still got to get her out and shoot her.'

Tanner grinned and shot a stream of tobacco juice past the ear of the nearside leader. 'Ain't that the truth?' he said. 'Ain't that the gospel truth? You lose much?'

'Enough,' Bligh growled grudgingly, and the driver was wise enough to leave it at that. He shook out the traces unnecessarily and chirruped at the leader, and the coach went spanking off down the long hill it had only recently laboured its way up.

The following morning, it was labouring its way up it again. This time, Bligh was sitting on the box with Tanner because he was the new guard, and the Greener was balanced across his knee. There was straight buckshot in both barrels and six pairs of cartridges in each pocket.

This time, too, they had another spare passenger, propped among the bags and trunks on the roof of the

Concorde. He was a spare, taciturn man with a battered sombrero, a leather jacket and a saddle which seemed to have come into the country with the Spanish conquistadors. His name was Emilio Chavez.

'You any good with that gun?' Tanner asked him, when he climbed aboard the Concord. Chavez gave him an opaque stare from black eyes as hard as hard as flint.

'*Si*,' he said without embellishment, and tucked the Winchester carbine between his knees, muzzle pointing skyward. It was a well-used weapon, but clean and bright and on Chavez it looked as though it had grown there.

With its six horses again, the Concorde climbed the long hill in good time, and Chavez asked as it got to the top: 'Where was it you were held up?'

'Right about here,' Tanner told him, as he sawed the traces to bring the horses' heads round to make the descent. 'He was behind that rock over there—'

'And here he is again!' roared the voice of the bandit, as the man with the grotesque mask came out from behind the boulder on the same horse and wielding the same weapons he had used on the previous day.

Tanner was caught with his hands full with traces, and the two new horses he had added to the team that morning still being a little fractious among their new teammates.

Bligh, however, was not. The Greener came up to waist height, and he let go with both barrels. The movement caught the bandit by surprise, but he tugged jerkily at the reins, pulling the horse back on its haunches.

His action turned its head as it reared, and the animal turned on its hind legs. The buckshot charge flickered past the rearing horse, one of the heavy balls scouring its

14

neck, and the animal hit the ground running like a jack-rabbit.

Somehow, the bandit managed to keep his seat, threw himself down along the horse's neck, and even two shots from Chavez's Winchester missed him. The horse, screaming like a hurt woman, went hell-for-leather out into the desert for the second time in forty-eight hours, and Tanner finally got his spooked team under control.

The stage racketed down the slope towards far away Tucson, and the hold-up was over.

It was not until he had reloaded the shotgun and wedged himself securely into his seat that Bligh realized he had also heard the sharp crack of the miniature Colt belonging to the girl during the exchange of shots. He wondered if she, too, had missed, or managed to score a hit, and if so, on which – rider or mount?

CHAPTER TWO

Charlie Shibell was a man of few words but he spent a surprising number of them cursing when he heard about El Mexicano's two hold-ups in two days. And when he heard about the injuries to Japhet the guard, he spent a whole lot more.

'Japhet's got a growing family,' he explained unnecessarily to Bligh and Tanner. 'He liable to be out of action for long?'

Tanner nodded his head seriously. 'Thought it was just a shoulder wound. But the doc back at the Wells sucked his teeth a heck of a long time when he looked at it. Don't know what that road agent was loading in his cartridges, but it cut poor Japhet up something cruel.'

Bligh agreed. The wound was not just a straight through bullet hole, but a messy, torn one and much of the man's shoulder blade had gone with it. The shock, too, had been serious. The unfortunate Japhet had not just taken a wound in the shoulder, he would be a cripple for the rest of his life.

'What do you think?' Shibell asked Bligh. 'You seen many bullet wounds?'

'Fair share,' Bligh told him laconically. 'This one's bad.

I reckon he cross-cut the nose of the shell. Wasn't no through-and-through, that's for sure.'

'Made a dum dum out of it, you mean?' Shibell asked. The deformed bullets spread out in the wound and did terrible damage, particularly if, like this one, they hit a bone. Similar bullets, called Minie balls, were feared and hated in the War Between the States, where they were almost always fatal, and left terrible, torn wounds which infected easily in the dreadful conditions of field hospitals.

'Same kind of thing,' Bligh agreed. 'Only knew of one man survived a body wound with one, though I heard it was not unknown. Always left a terrible wound, though.'

The purpose of such a slug was to kill, by infection if not from shock at first impact, and the three men sat for a few seconds in silence.

'You see anything else at all about him that would pick him out?' asked Shibell.

Bligh and Tanner went through their memories of the bandit, though Bligh privately thought they were telling the sheriff nothing new.

'Rode a paint pony, and it will have at least one wound in its neck, now. The buckshot grazed it,' Bligh opined. 'Can't tell you much about him personally. I never saw him off the horse, so I can't say whether he was tall or not. Powerful built man, though. Big shoulders, big arms, and he handled that big handgun easily enough.'

Tanner interrupted. 'Guns were easy to recognize, though,' he added. 'He used one of those ten-shot pistols. Looks like a cut-down saddle carbine, you know the ones? You have to reload every shot by working the lever.'

The rancher agreed with him and added that the bandit's rifle was easy to recognize, too. 'Must have got it off an Indian or an Indian trader. It was an old Henry with shiny studs all over the butt. Must shine like a dancehall girl's jewellery in the sun.'

The sheriff sat pinching his chin under his moustache. For a moment he looked perplexed.

'Funny thing, that,' he said eventually. 'Mostly road agents choose clothes you wouldn't pick out in a crowd. Hold-up men don't dress no different from ranch hands. Aren't many of them use distinctive weapons, either.'

'And none who rides a horse you could pick out at twenty miles in a sandstorm,' agreed Bligh. 'Good horses, sure. Makes for a quick getaway when things go bad. It was almost like this guy wanted to draw attention to himself.'

The more he thought about it, the more he found it odd. There were plenty of people around the Arizona Territory who wore fancy clothes. A Mexican rancher on a visit to town glowed like a lighthouse with studs and bright colours.

But the clothes and gear worn by El Mexicano were like a shout in a church. A blind man could hardly miss him.

'When you think about it,' he said slowly, 'It was like he wanted people to remember him, just like that.'

The grotesque mask, the showy, fancy outfit, the off-beat small arms, the horse which could not be missed – the more he thought about it, the more it looked as though he and the rest of the stage passengers were meant to remember the flamboyant outfit, and be distracted from its contents.

Shibell was watching him through narrowed eyes. 'Tell me what you are thinking,' he said. 'You got the same expression on your face my wife calls my "suddenly a great light dawns" look I get from time to time.'

Bligh explained his theory. 'He wants you to remember the outfit, the horse and the funny firearms,' he concluded. 'But none of us has looked through it to see the man inside. I sure didn't. Don't even know how tall he is, the colour of his hair, how old he is.'

And that meant the man had to disguise his appearance. Why should he, though? If he was a renegade hiding out in the mountains and the badlands, what did it matter who was able to recognize him?

On the other hand, a man who had changed his appearance to that extent could go where he wanted. He could walk into any saloon in the Territory and buy himself a drink, get his cartridges at Spangenberg's in Tombstone, his dinner at Delmonico's in Tucson.

He would in fact be invisible. It was almost frightening.

On the other hand.

On the other hand, a man who was used to being invisible would not bother to cover his tracks, because so far as he was concerned, he was leaving none. Nobody knew what he looked like out of his working clothes. So why would he bother to change or conceal his normal appearance?

How would anybody find him?

Bligh made his goodbyes to the sheriff and walked with Tanner down to the stage company's offices and picked up his wages for the trip as shotgun guard.

'You coming back to the Wells with me?' said Tanner. 'Can't take you as guard. Hank Marvell usually rides shotgun out of Tucson, and I'm bound to take him on this trip and back. But the company'll stand you the fare.'

Bligh shook his head and grinned. 'I got me a ride this far and my ranch is closer to here than it is to there,' he

19

said. 'Just shuck my saddle and traps out of the boot, and I'll get me a horse and ride on up home for a visit. Good to check on the place.'

He had no intention of going back to the ranch until he had at least tried to recover his money. Manolito, his cook and general caretaker, could go on looking after the buildings as he had during the drive to Yuma and the ride back. There were enough supplies out there to keep him alive and happy, and the old man was no sophisticate. A warm bed on cold nights and a cool patio on hot days kept him amused, and there was no Indian trouble at the moment to speak of, particularly since Manolito had as much Pima blood as he had Spanish.

Bligh humped his saddle over to the Wonton saloon and talked Bert, the barman, out of a room for the night. The two were old friends, and there was a room behind the storeroom next to the bar where he could stretch his bedroll and sleep undisturbed.

It was full dark when he awakened, and Tucson was just getting into its stride. In Tucson, the stride was long and very noisy, and he stripped to the waist and washed himself thoroughly in the washroom behind the bar. The water was cold, but there was a brick of soap which would have stripped paint if rubbed in too hard.

'One rub, no dirt: two rubs – no skin,' his mother used to say of homemade soap. Harsh, but it sure did get him clean when he was a kid and just as efficiently now.

There was a shirt in his blanket roll which was worn but clean, and he took the time and another rub of the frightening soap to wash his dirty shirt. Usually after a drive, he burned his old clothes and bought new. But usually, after a drive, he had money in his pocket.

He dug through his pockets and assembled enough cash combined with his wage as a shotgun man to see him through a good few days. In the sole of his boot, there was a small packet which contained sixty dollars in twenties: 'panic money', he called it, and if he was not exactly panicking now, he most certainly felt the money would not know the difference.

The night was fairly bouncing as he sat down at a table at the Palace in Congress Street, and ordered a steak and a beer. There was a new girl in town who had caused a sensation at the Birdcage in Tombstone earlier in the year by dancing in the manner of the Turkish belly-dancers. If she could brave the trigger-happy drunks of Allen Street, Tombstone, he reckoned she should handle Tucson easily enough.

In the event, it turned out he was to be disappointed in all respects. The much heralded belly dancer turned out to be a tubby girl wrapped in what looked like lace curtains, who wobbled her way on to the little stage, and wriggled frantically while the pianist tried to evoke the atmosphere of a Turkish harem.

If Turks were that badly off, Bligh thought, no wonder they made such ferocious fighters. He felt like running out into the street and shooting somebody himself.

But she was received readily enough by the rough crowd in the Palace, and wobbled, perspiring, off to loud applause.

As she went, he caught sight, out of the corner of his eye, of a man who was applauding enthusiastically and looking around himself as if to share the enthusiasm. It was not that he was actually familiar, Bligh thought. But there was something about him which caused a ripple in the mind.

He finished his meal, drank his beer and kept an eye on the stranger. The man was a big, well-built figure with prominent cheekbones and a goatee beard. He had a double breasted coat thrown over his shoulders, and a fancy waistcoat strangely out of keeping with what were after all rough working clothes.

There was nothing to distinguish him from eighty per cent of the rest of the men in the bar, and yet the very presence of the man made Bligh uncomfortable. He ordered another beer, and paid the stringy, red-headed waitress, when she brought the drink. As he did so, he accidentally caught the eye of the man at the bar and saw his expression change abruptly.

When he looked up the next time, the big man was gone. At the table where he had stood was a schooner of beer whose foaming top was slowly subsiding, and there was a cigar burning down on the big pot ashtray, but the man had vanished without leaving a ripple.

What had made him vanish, and was it coincidence that he had gone during the time Bligh's attention was distracted? Had he recognized Bligh from the hold-ups? If he was in fact El Mexicano, it was very likely that he had, but he must be aware that it would be impossible for any of his victims to identify him in return.

Bligh got up and went to the door. There were people sitting out on the sidewalk in the cool of the evening, and the usual passers-by. They were of course at this time of night almost exclusively men, for a respectable woman might be out on Congress Street in daylight, but she would not dream of risking it at night. Tucson could be a rough town.

He was distracted by shouting and watched one of the saloons further down the street belch a knot of soldiers on to the sidewalk. They were very drunk, and had got to the fighting stage, though luckily only with one another. Fort Lowell, the locals felt, was too close to the centre of town, and it was impossible to keep the army personnel out of the saloons.

Personally, Bligh did not mind their drinking habits. The blue-coat troopers got a pittance in pay, served in the kind of heat which would fry an egg on the breech of their guns in midsummer, and were often in more danger from their serving conditions than their opponents.

They were there to protect the Territory, but the reality of their service was frying heat and lurking sickness, with the occasional frenzied explosion of activity. Small wonder that when they could, they took to their fists and feet as a protest against their conditions.

Nevertheless, he prudently crossed the street and stepped into the doorway of one of the Mexican cantinas when the fighting looked like spilling his way. It was easier to be sympathetic if he did not get involved in an army fracas.

The cantina was much more quiet than the saloon across the street. There were a few round tables with stools, a big arched fireplace in the middle of the room open on both sides, which also doubled as a cooking fire. A couple of the tables were occupied and, to his surprise, he found Chavez sitting at one, eating.

The Mexican looked up as Bligh came in, and pointed at the stool opposite. When Bligh sat down, a girl brought a clay pot of wine and a thick glass tumbler. The wine was white and startlingly cool and good. He said so.

'It is made here,' Chavez told him. 'They have a vine-yard down towards Tubac, and it gives a good white grape. In this heat, you get an intense wine. Good flavour.'

He was drinking the same thing himself, and the two men talked wine for a half hour. Bligh had spent some of his military service in Mexico and was more used to drink-ing wine and particularly liked the cold Cucacmonga favoured by Arizonans.

Chavez finished his meal and mopped his plate with a scrap of bread. The girl brought him coffee and a cup for Bligh as well.

'You are looking for our visitor from Maricopa,' said Chavez, leaning forward to light his cigar from the candle on the table.

'You better believe it. I thought I saw him across the street, but he lit a shuck while I was not looking,' Bligh admitted.

'He came through here, just before you came in,' said Chavez.

'Big man, fancy vest and a bloodstain on his pants?'

The Mexican nodded calmly. 'The same. I thought he was familiar, as well. But I could not be certain.'

Bligh was looking around, carefully.

'Where is he?'

'Would such a man stay here? He entered, he crossed the room, he went. I thought there was that about him I recognized, but I could not be certain. Like you I never saw him dismounted, and his clothing was different. Now, I am.'

Bligh made to rise, but the Mexican waved him back to his stool.

'By now he has gone far away, or, worse, he is waiting for

you to come through that back door. Either way, to rush out would be pointless and, possibly, fatal.'

He pulled on the cigar until it was well alight, and drank some of his coffee.

'By good fortune, I know how to find him. But not until morning. So let us have more coffee, maybe another flask of wine. We have plenty of time.'

But Bligh was impatient. 'If you know how to find him in the morning, why not now? That bastard has my money, and I want it back,' he said. He slipped the thong off the hammer of his pistol, and made to rise again. Chavez sighed.

'In the morning, he will be taking his horse to the smith. It needs a new shoe on its off-side rear hoof. The animal shed its shoe when he held us up. For him to get here before us, he cannot have taken the horse to a smith between the hold up and the stage arriving, so it remains unshod.'

No outlaw would leave himself with a mount which needed a shoe. He could never be certain he would not need to make a quick getaway at a moment's notice. This outlaw must have at least two mounts, the paint pony and whatever horse he rode into Tucson. He would be certain to want both ready for flight.

'So, in the morning, he needs to take his paint to a smith. There is only one smith here in Tucson, and he lives over his smithy. He will not work at night, because the forge goes cold, and it will need to be relit and fed to bring it up to the right heat to make a shoe. Even if he has ready-made shoes waiting, they will need to be worked to fit the paint.'

He leaned back as though he had just run a long

distance, drew on his cigar and sent a plume of smoke towards the fireplace.

'He cannot move until morning, *amigo*. And in the morning, we will find him at the smithy. There, he will tell us where to find your money.'

Bligh sat down again, shrugged, and poured himself more wine. There was a logic in what the man said which brooked no argument.

CHAPTER THREE

The blacksmith was glad to see them in the dawn's early light. Indeed, he was overjoyed. He was sitting with his back to the massive wooden block on which his anvil was mounted, bound to the block with chains. His mouth had been stuffed with a rag so foul that it took him several minutes and a gallon of water to clear it enough to talk.

His language, when he could talk, would have dazzled the sheriff. Even Bligh, who had served in more than one cavalry outfit, was impressed. He did not even bother to express his own feelings, because he was certain he could not equal that of the smith.

'He was here, then?' he asked, when the smith paused for breath.

'Here and gone, the treacherous sidewinder,' the smith confirmed. 'No, he's worse than a rattlesnake. At least you can hear them coming. This bastard got me out of bed, promised me twice the money to shoe his horse, and drew down on me as soon as the job was done! If I see him again, I'll. . . .'

What he would do was inventive and sounded painful, but it also involved finding the bandit, and when they got

27

right down to it, he had no more idea where to look than they had.

'He come along with two horses, hours after I was in bed, and said he had to be in Phoenix come tomorrow night. Said it was a family matter and there would be a tragedy if he didn't make it.'

So the blacksmith, more for the money than the urgency, had got out of bed and dressed, heated up his forge and converted one of his stock horseshoes for the limping horse, which, yes, was a pretty paint pony. It had a wound on its neck, but only skin deep, he confirmed.

'I fixed that for him, too. Didn't need much, just a wash down with spirit. There wasn't no infection. You don't get that many in the desert. Horse was sore, but he ain't hurt bad. Won't even notice in a couple of days.'

He seemed more concerned with the horse's wound than the fact that he had been robbed, but he recovered his temper enough to make a pot of coffee, and threw hunks of bacon on to the back of a shovel to fry some breakfast.

'You searching for that guy? You make sure you find him,' he told them around a mouthful of bacon and camp-fire bread. 'That guy got no conscience a-tall. Nary one little bit.'

No, he had not noticed which way the man went, on account of he was chained to his own anvil at the time. Even his description of the bandit was vague. He had been big, yes, over six feet tall, and had a beard.

That could just as easily have been Sheriff Shibell, or Chavez, or even at a pinch, Tom Bligh himself after a few days on the trail. They had lost their quarry, and he had several hours' start on them.

The two men were making for the stables and corral to get themselves mounts when Bligh stopped dead in his tracks.

'Damn!' he said in an incredulous half whisper. Chavez stared at him, and raised his eyebrows.

'You think of something?'

'Rent me a horse, will you, Chavez? I don't need a saddle, mine's at the Palace. I'll meet you back there. There's something I got to check on before we go off on a mad monkey chase, and that smith might just recall it.'

He ran back to the smithy, just in time to stop the smith brushing out his workshop.

'Leave the floor just a minute, why don't you?' he said. 'There's something I got to look at. Something important.'

He knelt on the floor near the hitching rail where the horses were tied while the smith worked on their feet. The smith hung over the rail to watch, twitching with curiosity.

'What you looking for?' he said.

'Where was that little paint when you was working on his feet? Right here?'

'Just about. Yeah, there's the dirt I cleaned out of his hoof. Kind of reddish stuff just there, by the block. His hoofs was full of it. So was the other mount, now I recall. I checked them over while the sidewinder was here.'

Bligh leaned back on his haunches and ran the crumbs of earth through his fingers. They were still very slightly damp, which indicated they had been there less than a day. In Tucson's heat even in the spring days before the summer baked the earth, mud became dust within hours.

'Where would a horse pick up red mud coming down to your forge?' he asked the smith, and the man's face cleared.

29

'Santa Rita's got red mud upstream. Bert Clegg brings his wagon teams down the river when they need shoes. I'm always having to pick that red stuff out of their feet. There's a streak of red in the Santa Catalinas, too. Can't think of any others, though, right off the top of my head. Reckon that cheating coyote comes from up there, maybe?'

Bligh stood up, rubbing the remains of the red earth through his fingers He dug his tobacco sack out of his pocket, and wrapped a lump of the reddish mud in one of his cigarette papers.

'Can't say for certain, but it seems reasonable to me, friend. If his horses picked up mud it must have been on their way down here. That means this was wet last night. What time did he get you out of your blankets?'

The smith scratched his chest thoughtfully.

'Well, now, it was well after midnight, for the town was quieting down, and the lamps was out on the sidewalk down towards the old Spanish quarter. I reckon to have been in bed a couple of hours, at the least, and I wasn't early abed last night for once. Sat up playing cards with Charlie McCrory and a couple of guys till late.'

He yawned and scratched his chest again. 'Three in the morning, I reckon. Three or thereabouts. Yeah, had to be three, for the forge wasn't cold. I got her going again with the bellows in the embers. Say three to half after three. That help?'

Bligh heard hoofs approaching and glanced up to see Chavez had brought the horses. Bligh's saddle was already on the back of one of them, and his blanket roll packed on the back.

'How long did the work take?'

30

'Not long. Quarter-hour to get the forge up to heat. I cleaned out the horses' hoofs, say ten minutes, maybe another quarter hour. I trimmed the hoof that needed to be shod, that took fifteen at least, for that little paint sure was nervous. Heat up the shoe, five, shape it say another ten.

'No more than an hour, hour and a quarter, to do the shoeing, maybe another half hour treating that cut on his neck, for he didn't like that. How long is that?'

'Hour and fifty-some minutes, give or take,' said Bligh. 'Anything else?'

'Yeah, took him ten minutes to get me wrapped up in that chain, and he sure made a good job of it. I couldn't hardly breathe.'

'So he was here at least two hours?'

'I reckon. Yeah, two hours, tops.'

'And we was here round about dawn, say half past five, quarter to six? He wasn't gone more than a half, three-quarters of an hour when we got here?'

The smith shrugged. 'Must be about that.'

So the bandit was not more than six to ten miles way, according to whether he was hurrying or not.

Chavez was watching him thinking it through. Bligh grinned at him.

'The Santa Catalinas, I reckon,' he said. 'Maybe ten, fifteen miles. I know where that red mud came from, and that's where we'll start. Any luck, we'll catch the thieving skunk while he's having his breakfast.'

They crossed the Rillito river in shallow water and by pure chance, splashed ashore almost in the tracks of the two horses and their owner, who was angling easterly towards the mountains and, presumably, his hideout. The tracks were crisp in the mud and the new shoe the luckless smith had fitted showed up clearly.

In the scrub beyond the river, they lost him again, but picked him up by taking a line on the nearest and most obvious canyon in the range, and making for that.

The bandit and his horses were angling towards the big canyon the locals called Massacre Gulch and their path did not deviate.

'Either he don' know we're on his trail or he don' care,' opined Chavez, uneasily. 'He don' strike me as a man who gets careless, and don' watch his back trail. And if he don' care whether he's being followed or not, why not?'

The same thought had occurred to Bligh, but he pushed it to the back of his mind and concentrated on searching the rim rocks with his eyes for signs of an ambush. Even so, the first rifle report took him by surprise, and he and the hired horse were heading, belly down, for the shelter of a rocky outcrop. Chavez almost beat him to it, and both men dismounted and peered round the sides of the rock.

The shot was not repeated, and they waited for a while to see if anything else should happen. It was a still, hot day, but there was no sign anywhere of the smoke which would be left by a black powder cartridge, and after a few minutes, Chavez said what they were both thinking.

'I don' think he was shootin' at us, *amigo*,' he said. 'We was riding slow and in the open. If he was any sort of a shot, he would have hit us, I think.'

Bligh agreed with him, but the shot had been clear and not far away, and he could see no other target in the land-scape. However, a quick dash from the cover of the rock to another rock brought no more shots, and he decided Chavez had been right.

'The shot came from over towards that canyon, I think,' said Chavez. 'Maybe we try there.'

They separated and approached the cleft between two peaks from two directions, always keeping one another in sight, and both men rode with their rifles cocked and across their knees. Nothing more happened.

Together they arrived at the narrow entrance to the canyon, and paused.

'Cover me,' said Bligh, and Chavez nodded. One behind the other, they entered the narrow cleft.

Inside, the heat was concentrated by the steep walls. The air was still, and horses' hoofbeats sounded unnaturally loud in the confined space. Bligh rode loose in the saddle, Winchester in his right hand and pointing skywards, with its butt resting on his thigh.

Behind him, Chavez was moving cautiously. Every now and again, he swabbed his streaming forehead with a bandanna, but it was a losing battle. Out on the open ground, the heat was able to dissipate. Here it merely clung in like a burning blanket, and it was unrelenting.

They topped out in the pass without incident, and started to descend the other side, warily eyeing the rim above them for a waiting marksman.

Nothing broke the hot silence except the hoofs of their own horses.

It was not until the canyon started to open out again that Bligh picked up tracks. He had been dividing his attention between the rim above him and the trail he was following, and was aware that he might have missed some signs on the way, but the print of the new horseshoe on a patch of hard baked earth was unmistakable.

It looked as though the bandit was heading towards a long rise on the right of the trail, and although it apparently led nowhere, Bligh pointed at it with his rifle, and Chavez waved his own carbine to signify he understood.

He sat his horse at the bottom of the slope while Bligh concentrated on getting his horse up it safely. On the way, he caught sight of the tell-tale shoe several times, amid a confused mass of other hoofprints.

At the top, the slope divided to pass either side of a mass of tumbled rocks which seemed to have come down from the peak of the mountain ahead. Cautiously, Bligh moved his mount to pass to the right of the rocks, but even as he did so, Chavez, lower down the slope, whistled.

Bligh looked over his shoulder, to find the Mexican pointing urgently to the left of the rock pile. He seemed to be directing Bligh's attention to the slope further to the west.

Bligh turned his horse and backtracked until he could see past the boulders. Chavez kept pointing urgently and suddenly Bligh could see what he was trying to say. Further up the slope, almost hidden in the fringe of the rocks, he could now see a darker patch.

He dismounted and, leading the horse, he made his way up the side of the rock pile until he could see the darker patch more clearly. Even from this vantage point, he could not quite make out what it was, but it certainly was not a part of the rocky outcrop.

He heard Chavez riding up the slope behind him, and climbed back on to his horse, keeping his eye on the side of the rock pile, but there was no movement, and eventu-

ally he urged the horse up the hill until he could see properly.

To his amazement, it was a cleft in the rock which
opened up the closer he got to it, until he could see into
the darker interior, and make out that it was a shallow
cave, at the base of which was a pool of water. The horse
whickered and pricked up its ears when it caught scent of
the pool, and pulled at the reins.

Still suspicious, he restrained the animal and rode
forward until he could see clearly down into the tank. It
was a deep pool of clear water and he could see the rocks
at the bottom of it, very plainly.

At the side of the tank which was uphill of the water was
a patch of sand which ran down into the pool, and in it, he
could read the prints of the two horses they had been
following. The rider had stopped here to water his horses,
and from the boot prints in the little beach, to drink
himself and fill his canteen. There was another curious
other print in the sand which looked like the seat of a pair
of baggy pants.

'Water skins. He goes far,' Chavez said casually.

Chavez seemed to be a practised tracker. Bligh could
see the shape of the skins clearly now they had been identified, and he stared at them for a while, memorizing the
baggy, creased look of the print. When he saw them again
he would know them.

'So he stopped here,' he said, looking back down the
mountain and towards Tucson, where columns of smoke
rose into the clear desert air, and wobbled from the heat
refraction. If the bandit had stopped there within the last
couple of hours, he would have been able to see his
pursuers coming across at least a part of the open land.

Further away towards the town the terrain was too broken to be certain, but down on the skirts of the mountain, they would have been easy to spot, if only from their dust trail on the still air.

'He could have seen us,' Chavez confirmed. 'But he must know he is pursued. Already he acts like a quarry. He has his horse shod for the journey. It is an easy beast to spot, so to bring it into town at all is a risk. Yet he does it, even when he must have seen you in the saloon. He runs.'

Together they looked up the mountain again, and Bligh shrugged. 'The guilty flees when no man pursueth,' he agreed.

'*Que?*' Chavez peered at him under the wide brim of the sombrero, and he grinned.

'Means a man with a guilty conscience runs even when he ain't being chased,' Bligh explained. The Mexican's eyebrows knitted.

'But he is being chased. We chase him,' he protested.

'Yeah,' said Bligh. 'Ain't he the guilty one, then? It was just something my grandma used to say when we was kids.'

Chavez looked a little like a man who has run into a low beam, in the dark, then shook his head and pointed up the hill.

'He goes that way. Now we can chase him,' he said decisively and Bligh grinned and nodded.

'Ain't that the truth?' he said, and led off up the hill, leaning over to one side to follow the tracks of the fugitive.

CHAPTER FOUR

They found the paint pony within the next hour. It had been shot, once, in the head and had died where it fell. The new shoe gleamed in the sunlight and the scar on its neck confirmed its identity if they had needed it.

Chavez swore when he saw it, and looked bitter.

'*Pobrecito!*' he said, and spat disgustedly into the dust.

'What's the matter?' Bligh asked him, puzzled.

'I like horses,' the Mexican told him. 'This one died for nothing. The man is afraid it will identify him, and we already know what he looks like.'

It made a brutal kind of sense, but it also deprived them of their most reliable trail setter, and they both knew it.

'Best try to find the tracks of the other horse,' Bligh said, casting his mind back to the tracks in the river bank and at the water-hole. But the paint with its new shoe had left a reliable and distinctive track, and the other horse, presumably the bandit's favourite mount, had worn shoes with no particular distinguishing marks.

From what the smith had said, El Mexicano's other horse was a big chestnut with a white blaze on its forehead, but the description hardly distinguished it from a dozen horses which could be found at the average hitching rail. Even its shoes had no characteristic marks.

'Why did he kill this horse just here, *amigo*?' said Chavez suddenly. 'Why have him shod, then bring him up here and shoot him? What does he gain?'

Bligh dismounted and hunkered down near the dead horse. From the few faint tracks in the dust, the bandit had ridden the two horses up here, pulled a gun and shot the paint, then left him where he fell. There were footprints in the dust around the horse, as though the man had performed some important task next to it, then remounted and ridden off.

'Bandit was just getting rid of evidence and now he has a fresh horse to travel,' he said 'We seen this horse at the hold-up and the smith seen him with El Mexicano. He's like a birthmark. You can't change him and everybody remembers him.

'I reckon he just chose this horse because he's easy to remember and he only ever rode him when he was on the owlhoot trail.'

Chavez nodded. 'So where we go from here?'

Bligh stood up and looked round carefully. They were in a narrow valley which dropped down from the crest of the mountain and opened into the land to the east of Tucson. It was broken ground with an evil reputation, because it offered ready cover for outlaws within easy reach of the railroad, the town and its saloons, and an easy getaway into the hills.

'I reckon he's heading for the badlands south of here,' he said. 'Maybe even as far down as Tombstone. He can follow the San Pedro down that wash so he'll have water and cover.'

'If he can get to it,' grunted Chavez. 'He might have run into trouble.'

Bligh looked at him in surprise. 'Trouble?' he said. 'What kind of trouble.'

'This kind,' said Chavez, who was looking over his head towards the lower end of the valley. Bligh followed his gaze and swore softly. Coming up the valley were three horsemen, and Bligh knew just what Chavez meant by 'trouble'.

The leader of the group reined in his horse when he was still some yards from them, and sat watching them. He was a thin faced, stoop shouldered man in a leather vest and jeans, and his wool shirt was soiled around the neck.

He wore a glove only on his left hand, which held his reins, and his right rested on his thigh, where it was only inches from the butt of his gun. Behind him the other two men reined in crowded by the narrow trail.

They looked what they were: bad men with guns. Their horses were good riding stock with broad shoulders and deep chests, and though their riders' clothing was shabby and dirty, their weapons were oiled and polished and looked in excellent condition.

They had the same hard, tanned faces and the same stooped shoulders, and their eyes looked out on the world as though through loopholes in a wall.

'Howdy,' said the leader, around the cigar butt which seemed to have been nailed to the side of his mouth. Chavez and Bligh nodded, watchfully. They did not speak.

'Come far?' He showed no sign of embarrassment at their silence.

'Fair step,' Bligh told him, and remounted his horse. The move put him slightly higher than the newcomers, and they did not like it. One of the men, at the back, began to move his horse around, uneasily. Under cover of the movement, his hand slipped down towards his hip.

'Going far?'

'All the way,' Bligh told him. He was watching the restless horseman carefully. The slowly moving right hand was almost at the hip, now.

'All the way, huh? Reckon you'll make it all the way?'

'Sure am,' said Bligh. 'Which is more than your friend there will do if he don't take his hand away from that gun.'

The leader did not bother to look over his shoulder. A tight grin started to spread across his face.

'Why, what's gonna to happen to him?' he asked and the taunt in his voice was obvious.

Bligh grinned. 'Why, he's gonna finish up wearing his shirt buttons on his backbone,' he said gently.

Behind him he could hear the crisp click as Chavez cocked his carbine, and a guarded look came over the rider's face.

'Now, you hang on a minute there,' he protested. 'No call for you to throw down on us. No call for hard words between men as meet on the same trail, neither. Just passing the time of day, that's all. Just a bit of talk on the trail.'

Chavez said from behind Bligh: 'Well, you talked. Pass on.'

There was a flicker in the thin man's eyes, and Bligh knew the fight was inevitable. He jumped his horse at the leader, crashing into the man's shoulder as he grabbed for his gun.

The man's horse tried to rear out of the way, but was caught against the side of the trail, and slipped, throwing its rider off balance, and making him grab for the saddle horn.

The two men behind were crowded by the rearing horse, and Bligh heard at least one shot in the mêlée. He slashed sideways with his pistol, catching the nearer rider on the cheekbone and knocking him out of his saddle.

Behind him he could hear Chavez's rifle banging away like a cannon, and the tail end man who had been reaching for his gun somersaulted over his horse's rump, with blood spouting from his neck.

Bligh swung the horse around, pistol poised, and found he had no targets to shoot at. The leader was lying in the trail pawing at a broken leg, while his horse kicked against the side of the defile, spooked by the shooting.

Chavez threaded his way through the mess, rifle poised for a shot, but none was required. The leader was down, and the one he had knocked out of the saddle lay against a rock with his neck at an impossible angle. His horse stood nearby, ground hitched and waiting for its owner.

Chavez said, '*Nombre de Dios*! What was that all about?'

The man with the broken leg was trying to reach his gun, but Bligh leaned down and knocked it beyond his reach. The man snarled at him.

'Why make a fight?' Bligh asked him. All he got in answer was a barrage of abuse. The horse had calmed down, now. Its rider had given up trying to reach his gun, and lay quiet.

'You come in here after us, law dog, you get all the trouble you can handle and then some, mister,' he said.

Chavez raised an eyebrow. 'Seems to me you are the one with the troubles, *hombre*. Who tell you we come after you? I never heard of you; I don't even know who you are now.'

The gunman sneered, though the effect of the sneer

was spoiled by his sudden yell of pain.

'I can smell a lawman five miles away, upwind. You're the law, mister. Don't try and tell me you ain't!'

Chavez shrugged. 'OK, I don' tell you I ain't. I still don' know who you are and why you draw down on us. Keep your secret, little man. You going to need all the luck you can get.'

He turned his horse away down the trail, and Bligh fell in beside him as they dropped down the hillside. The shouts of the frustrated bandit echoed after them, but neither man looked back.

They made the trouble, they can clear themselves up, Bligh told himself, and found he was in total agreement with his comment. It was not, he had to admit, unusual.

Chavez seemed troubled, nonetheless. Once or twice he turned in his saddle to look back at the ambush site.

'Something bothering you, Chavez?' Bligh asked, in the end. 'You keep looking back, and so far as I can make out, there ain't nothing to see.'

The Mexican shrugged. 'They were waiting for us,' he said. 'That was not just a fight on the road, and neither you nor I, *hombre*, look like we are carrying a bank vault in our saddle-bags. Why pick a fight with two strangers out here in the saguaros?'

He was right, and they rode on in silence for a while, though Bligh constantly searched the skyline and they veered away from any obvious cover. Bligh noticed that Chavez was being as watchful as himself.

Finally, with night falling, they stopped in a little rock-bound cove on the mountainside and heated water for coffee. Chavez produced a skillet, mixed flour and water, and started to make tortillas. With bacon and some beans they made a good meal.

'Tell me something,' Bligh said to him through a mouthful of food. The Mexican shot him a glance over the fire.

'Ask away, *amigo*,' he said.

'Who in the hangment are you?' The Mexican's eyes slid away from his, and Bligh hoped he had not misjudged the moment.

'I am Emilia Rodrigo de Chavez,' the Mexican said. 'Who do you think I am?'

Bligh used a cactus spine to pick a morsel of bacon out of his teeth. He was careful to keep his hands well away from his rifle, lying against a rock.

'I don't know, *amigo*,' he said. 'That's why I'm asking. Emilio Rodrigo de Chavez you may well be, but you are also almighty good with a gun, and you know when to use it. Your clothes ain't range tramp rig. Your guns are better than average. You just happen to be on a stagecoach which is robbed twice in two days, and you are on hand to help me run down the robber.

'What I want to know is: was you on that coach just by pure dumb luck, or was you there because you're looking for something or somebody? And if so, did you find him?'

Chavez leaned forward to the fire, and Bligh tensed, but the man was merely reaching for a burning twig to light his cigar. He pulled once or twice to get it lit, then blew out a long, perfect plume of smoke into the still air.The smoke was a startling white against the darkness.

'Well, *amigo*,' said the Mexican. 'You are right and you are wrong. I truly am Emilio Chavez, and I truly am from Mexico. What I did not tell you was that I am Teniente Emilio Chavez. I am one of the officers whose job is to patrol the border, and my particular responsibility is to make sure that our criminals do not cross into the Territories to stir up troubles, and that yours stay out of our country.'

He brushed the ash off the end of his cigar with a careful finger, and shook a few flakes off his shirt front.

'I have to admit, *amigo*, that I have had more successful enterprises in my life. I ride the border ceaselessly, but there are times when I feel that I might just as well have stayed at home and raised cows like my brothers.

'Everybody crosses when and where he wishes. The Apache raid south and hide north, then they raid north and hide south. The Sierra Madre is as full of them as a dog has fleas. They bite and they disappear. And the Americano are nearly as bad.'

'But this ain't an Apache,' protested Bligh. 'He's a Mexican himself. They even call him El Mexicano.'

'*Si*,' agreed Chavez. 'But he is not. He is a *gringo*. I excuse myself for using the term. Like all the rest, he raids south and hides north, then raids north and hides south. He is very successful both sides of the border. And we are getting very angry with him.' He pronounced the word: 'heem' which Bligh was beginning to recognize as a sign of deep irritation.

If Chavez was a border officer, a virtually impossible task since the border was new, mountainous and long, then he was probably being blamed for El Mexicano's continued success. It was likely that what had driven the officer north was desperation as well as his job.

There was also, at the back of Bligh's mind, the disturbing thought that El Mexicano was heading for the Dragoons, north of the new boom mining town of

Tombstone. Bligh's ranch, the Circle B, was precariously placed in those mountains, surrounded by rocks, cactus, and the traditional homeland of Apaches.

The efforts of the US Army to pacify and control them seemed to be having an effect, which made Tombstone and, to a lesser degree the Circle B, workable.

Granted, at the moment, the Apaches were quiet, which meant that nobody had provoked them into furious action, but all the situation needed was some provocative act on behalf of some foolhardy white man, and the whole area could turn back into a battleground.

Was El Mexicano capable of doing that?

'Does a bear shit in the woods?' Bligh asked himself grumpily as he rolled into his blankets. Chavez, who had drawn the short straw, took first watch, and for a long time, the camp in the boulders was a still and a silent place broken only now and again by the muffled sound of a horse blowing dust out of its nostrils in the night.

CHAPTER FIVE

The morning came up like a cavalry charge, the mountains to the east lighted from behind, and standing out in stark contrast to the glory of the sky. Bligh bent over his little fire, and blew the flames into enthusiasm under the coffee pot.

Chavez rolled out of his blankets without a word, shook out his boots and banged them together in case something venomous had taken shelter in there during the night, and stretched his arms above his head to iron out the overnight knots.

'*Hola, amigo,*' he said eventually. 'Good morning.'

Bligh, who was not a good man in the early mornings, grunted, and laid a knife blade by the coffee pot to see if it was boiling. The blade vibrated, so it was. He lifted the top off, and dashed in a handful of coffee grounds. The smell of coffee was delicious on the morning air.

During the night, the desert had yielded up its warmth and there had been a light frost. There was still a faint coating of it on the rocks, and Chavez laid his blanket on one before he sat down. He looked irritatingly cheerful.

'I sleep well in the desert,' he said, sipping at his coffee. 'It is, I think, the cold of the night. In more civilized places, there is no frost in the night, and I sweat in my blankets. In the desert, frost yes, sweat, no. I prefer it.'

He produced a length of stick, mashed the end flat with the pommel of his knife and used it to brush his teeth. It seemed to make his smile even more brilliant than usual. Bligh did his best not to scowl. He had used sand to clean his own, and the grains were still gritty on his mouth.

He swilled his teeth with a precious mouthful of coffee, then spat it out and refilled his cup. His chin was stubbly before he started and, in any case, any man who has ridden on a cattle drive became accustomed to a beard in short order. Water was far too precious to waste shaving.

Chavez walked over and checked on his horse, examining its hoofs for thorns and stone, and soothing the animal with a few pats on the neck and by stroking its nose. The horse seemed to appreciate the attention and blew noisily in his ear.

He walked back to the fire, bent to help himself to more coffee, and said in a low voice as he bent, '*Indios, amigo.* To the west. They watch us.'

Bligh grinned and nodded. 'I know. I seen them a half-hour since. They're Chiricahua Apaches on their way up from the Border. I reckon they overnighted about a mile to the east, and come upon us in the dawn.'

'But will they not attack?'

'If they was going to, they'da done it by now. Looks like the treaty's being observed both sides. Just pray some trigger-happy yahoo don't take a pop at 'em from pure fear or devilment.'

Chavez agreed, and the next time he looked, the Indians were gone. He drank more coffee, and ate some beans and camp-fire bread. They were good, and he said

47

so. Bligh nodded.

'Plenty of practice with a skillet and beans, *amigo*. Cattle drive I just finished was my fourth, and the cook died on the third one. Somebody had to cook, and the other boys didn't know which way up to hold the pan.'

They poured the coffee grounds on the fire and kicked sand over the dead embers.

'Where to, now?' Chavez asked as they mounted up.

'I been thinking about it,' said Bligh. 'That man's on the run, but he don't like being out of his own territory for long. Knows all the bolt-holes and the hide-aways, I guess. And I'll lay a miner's poke to a plugged nickel he's got a hideout around here. He had to keep that paint pony someplace.'

'True,' said Chavez. 'So where will he go now? He needs to be somewhere for the heat to cool off.'

'I think he's going to make for Tombstone to lie up for a while and get some grub and maybe a spare mount. He's got plenty of money with him. Mostly mine.

'After that, he could go south to the border, but I think he'll break back north to his familiar range. We can stop off at the Circle B and get fresh horses, then go on south to Tombstone. I reckon we'll find him there.'

But it was not that simple. In the Dragoons, nothing ever was, and Bligh bitterly reminded himself of that when they rode down out of the hills into the valley where Dragoon Springs Station stood.

The station was the local base for the stage line, and built like a small fort. There was a high wall around the compound, which contained the stables and the station buildings. The coaches came in through a high arched gateway at one side of the compound, and it had been intended that it should go out through a similar gateway at the far side.

But the far gate had never been built, and the wall stood unbroken. The compound was large enough for the coach to turn round, and the stables could take two teams of horses at once. Outside, there was a corral with a drinking trough for the livestock.

The stable hand was a Pima Indian whose understanding of horses was legendary, and the agent's Mexican wife handled what cooking the stage passengers required. They did not expect much, and they were not surprised, for though she could cook steak, tortillas and beans, she was a stranger to any cookery which did not involve chillies. Passengers claimed that eating a volcano would have much the same effect as Maria's chillies.

There was no food for the travellers today, however. The big Concord coach which was in the yard of the station, stood empty, and the horses were missing from the stables and the corral.

Chavez dismounted and examined the tracks in the ground by the single gate. Bligh walked round the compound carefully, sticking to the wall to avoid messing up any tracks, and entered the station building. It was silent and empty of life and, after listening for a moment, he shouted, 'Anybody home?'

Immediately, there was a sound of pounding and muffled shouting which came from behind the bar, and he leaned over to stare down at the floor.

In the middle of the bartender's walk between bar and wall there was a large trapdoor made of stout baulk of wood. The heavy steel bolt which secured it had been shot firmly home, and wedged into place with a cask of beer. It was too heavy for Bligh to shift by himself, and it had been wedged into place so that he could not tip it on its rim and roll it. He went to the compound, shook out his rope and led the horse into the bar room.

He shouted the prisoners below the trap into silence, explained he was about to let them out, and harnessed the horse to the beer barrel.

The horse towed the cask out of the way, and he was able to shoot back the bolts. When he called out that it was cleared, the trap opened cautiously and people began to emerge.

First up was the station man, reputed to be able to drop a horse with one blow of his fist and a man with one blow of his breath. There was a price to be paid for a diet based mainly on chillies. He was called Harry Wilson.

Behind them were the Pima station-hand, a married couple in go-to-town clothes, a large man in black broadcloth clothes sadly mired with desert dust – and Frankie Lewis.

She emerged from the hole in the ground dusting herself off and shaking the dirt out of her hair and blinking madly in the light. When she saw Bligh, she stared openly.

'Well, hello you!' she exclaimed delightedly and suddenly became self-conscious about her appearance, making for the door at the back of the bar room. Maria opened it for her and the other woman hurried through after her.

'Isn't that just like women the world over?' said the big man in broadcloth delightedly. 'Spend eight hours in a hole in the ground, and the first thing I think of is a big shot of whiskey and a smoke, first thing they think of is their hair! Howdy-doodie there, men. I'm Manfred Gilbourne, Gilbourne Enterprises.'

He was a hand-shaker and a hugger. As he shook hands with each of his rescuers, he also wrapped an arm round their shoulders and slapped them heartily on the back. Chavez surreptitiously checked his purse.

'Now, how soon can we get a new team of horses up here and that there Concord on the road?' Gilbourne was an organizer, and he did not mind who knew it.

Wilson was checking the bar and his wife was making noises in the kitchen which indicated that her pans and plates had been interfered with. She was a woman of high temper, and the nervous look on her husband's face betrayed the fact that he was usually the target of it.

The Pima had slipped away through the gate as soon as he came above ground, and Bligh assumed he had gone in pursuit of the horses. Chavez stepped outside and brought their mounts into the stables.

The women came back into the room having performed the female miracle of repair, and Maria disappeared again into the kitchen, to scarify some chillies.

Gilbourne took off his jacket and slapped it mightily against the edge of the bar, raising a small cloud of dust, When he had finished it did not look much better, but he seemed satisfied and called for whiskey. Wilson passed him a bottle and a handful of glasses, and brought coffee for the ladies.

'So what happened?' asked Bligh.

'Come in on the coach last night, round about sundown. Driver and the guard got down to open the gates, on account of they was closed, and drove the coach into the yard,' said Gilbourne, who was doing his best to revive a sadly crushed cheroot from his vest pocket.

'Lamps were all lit in the saloon here. Coffee pot in the kitchen on the stove. We called for the agent and his wife, and we got two men with guns, instead. Guard tried to get his shotgun into line, but they shot him. Driver was taken away, and we were all herded down into the cellar. Wilson and Mrs Wilson were already down there. And the Indian. Lamp gave out around midnight, I reckoned. Been in the dark ever since.'

For a man who had been held up and locked into a cellar he did not seem much fazed by events. He got his cheroot alight in the end, and poured himself more whiskey.

The Mexican woman brought food and coffee and put it on the table and they all settled down to a quick meal. It was bacon and beans with the inevitable chilli and Bligh and Chavez fell to with enthusiasm along with the passengers. The travellers talked excitedly about the hold-up, but the talk did not really amount to much that had not already been said.

The bandits had been waiting when they arrived in the dusk. The guard had been shot almost immediately and his body dragged off to one of the outhouses, where it still was. The driver had disappeared, and the opinion of Gilbourne at least was that he had been in league with the bandits, and probably made his escape with them.

The other passengers did not seem too happy with this idea, and the rancher's wife, after introducing herself and her husband as Cole and Winnie Bedford, openly pooh-poohed it.

'They were after the strongbox, and they said so,' she

said. 'The driver wouldn't give them the key and they took him away to beat the living daylights out of him. He can't have given them the key even then, because they must have taken the box with them, and it would be an awkward load to pack on a horse. I think we should search the buildings.'

With a glare at Gilbourne, she vanished into the kitchen without another word, and Wilson cocked his head at the sound of hoofbeats in the yard and went out of the doors. Frankie shrugged resignedly and went behind the bar to help herself. Bligh was not particularly surprised to see she favoured a glass of beer. She poured it expertly, blew the foam off the top like a practised barfly and sank half of it without taking a breath. As she put the glass down, she caught the eyes of the men in the room on her.

'What?' she said in a surprised voice. 'Why are you all staring at me?'

'Ain't seen a lady drink beer like that,' explained the rancher.

'Like what? Like I enjoyed it? Well, I do enjoy it and after eight hours in that stinking hole in the ground, I reckon I earned it, too. Cheers, boys!' and she sank the remainder of the beer and finished with a long sigh of satisfaction.

Bligh decided he liked this woman more every time he saw her, but he was worried about the missing stage driver. He took his rifle, shot a glance at Chavez and got a nod of understanding, then went out into the compound to search.

The Pima was bringing in two pairs of horses, riding one and trailing others by lead reins, and from the stables

Bligh could hear the sound of hoofs. Wilson was tending to two more horses, and he nodded at Bligh.

'Not hard to find them. There's a water-hole not far off, and any strays just naturally seem to head there,' he said. He jerked his head at the Pima. 'He can track a fly across a bar room, and he'll have them all back here before long.'

Bligh explained he was looking for the driver, and why. Wilson looked surprised.

'I kind of thought he must have gone with them. Maybe he's in the hay loft?' he asked. 'I ain't seen him no place else.'

Together, they mounted the stair into the hay loft, and poked in the hay. They found the driver in the corner, hidden behind some piles of hay. He had been bound hand and foot, and gagged, and he was unconscious. They untied the gag, loosed his hands and feet and carried him down the ladder and into the cooling dusk. He had been hit over the head, and was only just regaining proper consciousness.

'Lie still, Brad. I'll get Maria to come and look at that head wound before we move you,' said the station man, and disappeared. They could hear him shouting in the compound, and in a little while he came back with his wife, who was carrying a bowl, a jug of water and some bandages.

She examined the wound, and cleaned it. From the bosom of her dress she produced some herbs and pounded them into a paste which she laid on the wound and bound into place with a strip of cloth. The driver lay quiet while she was working, but started to struggle up when she had finished. She pushed him back on to the hay and scowled.

Her husband finished working on the horses, and came over to talk to her. They rattled on in Spanish for a moment, then he turned to the driver.

'Maria doesn't reckon you're in a fit state to drive, Brad,' he said. 'Best you stay here until the next stage comes through and go on with that. Somebody else can take this 'un through to Tombstone.'

Brad looked disposed to argue, then sank back on to his hay couch with a groan.

'Don't matter how you feel, you're staying here,' said Wilson. He was far too big to argue with, and the driver conceded. Together, they carried him across the compound to the main building, and put him into a bunk.

The passengers watched the progress, and their unhappiness was written on their faces. Unsurprisingly, it was Gilbourne who made the fuss.

'Why is that man staying in bed?' he asked loudly. 'This a stage line or a hospital? I need to get to Tombstone, and I need to get there right now! I have been held up for long enough, due to this stage-line!'

Wilson turned to face him. The two men were of a size, and Bligh realized that in a fight, he was not at all sure which would win. Harry Wilson was a renowned bare knuckle fighter, and immensely strong, but when he looked at Gilbourne, Bligh realized he was looking at a man who was not only strong, but would not hesitate to kill. It was written all over his face, and his right hand was hidden by the skirts of his coat.

'Back off, both of you,' he growled. 'I can drive a six-in-hand, and I know the trail down to Tombstone. The Indians are peaceful at the moment, so unless we run into the same two *hombres* held up the station, we should have a clear run. That OK by you, Harry?'

The station agent grunted, and nodded, but he stepped back from the confrontation with Gilbourne without taking his eyes from the man, and Bligh realized that Wilson, too, had noted the concealed right hand and was taking no chances.

He hitched his horse to the back of the coach, and they checked the passengers' baggage, which had all been opened and rifled through. The strong box was missing and presumably had been the target. The driver was drifting off to sleep, but roused himself to say fuzzily he had no idea what was in it, but it was heavy.

Bligh had been looking towards Gilbourne as he asked the question, and thought he saw a ripple of expression cross the big man's broad face. Exactly what it meant, he did not know, but that box meant something to Gilbourne, he was sure.

Frankie Lewis riffled through her looted bag. She moaned over some roughly handled lacy garments, and started to hold them up to see the damage better, then glanced round the room at interested male eyes watching her, and rolled them into a ball before stuffing them into her valise. When she caught Bligh's eye, she winked and grinned like a schoolgirl.

'You are a lucky man, I think,' Chavez murmured into his ear, as he checked the dead guard's shotgun. 'She likes you.'

Wilson stopped by the coach as Bligh gathered up the traces. He put one foot on the hub and leaned close to Bligh's ear.

'Watch that dude,' he said quietly, jerking his head at Gilbourne who was stowing his bag in the rear boot of the coach. 'He carries a derringer in his sleeve and he has a holster under his coat. They didn't take either weapon off of him last night, and he never made any attempt to pull one, neither. I don't trust him.'

He dropped to the ground as Chavez climbed up on the opposite side of the seat. The Mexican had taken on the role of the guard without being asked, tethered his horse, too, to the back of the coach and after helping the ladies into the vehicle, he threw the shotgun up on to the box and clambered up after it.

'*Vamos, amigo,*' he said, and flashed a grin at Maria, who had come to the door of the station to see them off. Bligh was surprised to see her face light up as she smiled in return and waved.

'I think you made a hit there, friend,' he said, as he shook out the traces and chirruped at the horses. Then he caught sight of Harry Wilson watching from the stable doorway. The man's face was thunderous.

'And just be sure he doesn't follow up by making a hit on you!'

The stage rattled out into the road and set off south for Tombstone.

CHAPTER SIX

The first part of the journey was uneventful. Despite Bligh's distrust of the man, Gilbourne remained quietly good-humoured.

The ladies chuckled at his jokes, and even the men relaxed a little as the journey passed. The stage route took a roundabout way to Tombstone, skirting the Dragoons to the north, but Bligh had been this way before, many times, and knew the stretches to take carefully and the parts where the road was comparatively level and could be trusted.

The big Concord coach was a pleasure to drive.

The horses sensed an unfamiliar hand on the traces right from the start, but they calmed down when Bligh made the whip dance about their ears, snapping and cracking like a Chinese cracker, and pulled away willingly enough.

All the same, Bligh was uneasy on the road, and he noticed that Chavez held the shotgun constantly across his knees and searched the countryside with more than usual care.

They made a water stop at a small creek on their way down from the mountains, and Bligh, who knew it was the last between him and Tombstone, let them drink. The horses whickered at him gently as he took them each a bucket of water in turn, he stroked their velvet noses and smacked reprovingly at the off leader which made a playful attempt to bite, though he was careful to stay away from its hoofs.

Chavez said: 'Something is hiding in those rocks up ahead. Twice that cactus wren tried to land, but he sheered off at the last moment. He does not like those rocks, *amigo*, and he should. Such rocks are full of good things for birds.'

Also of things like snakes, coyotes and wildcats, but the wren would know more about that than he did. Bligh handed Chavez a box of cartridges under cover of checking the traces, and nodded.

'I seen him balk at it, too. We'll swing wide.' Then he raised his voice for the passengers. 'We're going off the road here, ladies and gents. Be a mite bumpy for a while, so hold on tight.'

He pulled on the traces, and steered the team off the road and away from the rocks which had alarmed the wren. For a moment, he thought he saw a flicker of movement there, but no shot rang out and no bandit challenged the racing coach. After a short detour, he steered back on to the road, and grinned when he heard the shouts of approval from behind him.

They bowled into Tombstone before dusk, and trotted down Allen Street to stop at the Wells Fargo office. The dust swirled as he pulled the horses to a standstill, and the loafers come to the edge of the sidewalk to watch the passengers climb down. The arrival of a stage was always

59

an event in Western towns, and in Tombstone, just the fact that this one was late indicated there was a story to be had.

Gilbourne started telling it as soon as he got down from the stage. He seemed to have taken over care of the other passengers, calling for help in finding accommodation and refreshment for his fellow travellers, and sending volunteer loafers to collect their baggage and bring it along to the office.

Bligh and Chavez jumped from the box and helped the ladies down, and Bligh handed over what surviving mail there was to the agent, and then drove the coach round to the corral. Chavez had already found another corral for their horses, and they humped their saddles to the Cosmopolitan, a few doors down, where they got rooms and found that the Earps, currently the law in Tombstone since their now famous gunfight with the local group known as the Cowboys at the OK Corral, already knew about El Mexicano.

'Come through on the telegraph two days ago,' Art Knowles, the deputy, told him. 'Where you been since then?'

Bligh recounted the hold-up at Dragoon Station, and told him where to find the passengers he had brought in. He hesitated over reporting their moment of unease on the trail, but in retrospect it seemed to be too slight to mention.

'Earp will want to know the details. Where you bunking?' Knowles asked him. Bligh was surprised the Earps' jurisdiction extended out that far, and said so, but Knowles grinned and winked at him.

'Extends as far as they want it to, truth to tell,' he said. 'Wyatt's a clever man, and a clever man is one who knows what's going on. Wyatt likes to know what's going on.'

It made sense, right enough, and they told the deputy where to find them, and went along to the Maison Doree for supper. It was crowded and noisy, but they found themselves a corner table and ordered steaks and eggs. Chavez asked for a bottle of wine, and the waiter brought them glasses and a beer for Bligh, whose throat felt as though it had been living on a diet of dust for a week.

The food was good, as it should be in a town in the middle of a cattle area. It reminded Bligh of his own lost herd money, and he ate with a bitter taste at the back of his throat.

Chavez leaned back in his chair when they had finished and lighted a cigar.

'Does something strike you as being a little strange with this town?' he asked, looking round the room under his eyebrows. Bligh nodded.

'How come we haven't seen the coach passengers since we got here?' he said, and the Mexican nodded.

'It is the closest eating house to the office, and it seems to me to have a good reputation. Yet we have not seen the passengers, and particularly not our very noisy passenger with the big, black coat,' he said. 'Shall we go look for them, *amigo?*'

They left the café and stepped off the sidewalk, pushing their way among the horses at the hitch rail. The town was full, and there was a sound of jangling pianos coming from half a dozen saloons and gambling houses within the first hundred yards.

In front of the Birdcage Theatre, men were wrangling over the cost of entertainment, and from somewhere down towards the miners' cabins to the south, there came confused shouting, and then a shot. Nobody even turned his head towards the sound.

They pushed their way into a half-dozen saloons along the street before they came across the rancher and his wife, eating sedately in a restaurant.

'Evening, Mr Bedford, Mrs Bedford.' Bligh tipped his hat. The Bedfords smiled and nodded and Bedford asked him how thing had gone with the marshal.

'Told the deputy about the situation up at Dragoon, and he seemed interested enough. But, of course, it's out of his jurisdiction,' Bligh explained. 'Wells Fargo are sending a new team up there. Should be off first thing.'

He asked after Frankie Lewis, and was surprised to see their faces straighten. Mrs Bedford looked away and coloured slightly.

'She's ... er ... gone back to her old profession,' Bedford mumbled at last, and Bligh stared at him, amazed.

'You don't mean she's—?' he started, and the rancher's wife nodded, her eyes cast down on to the tablecloth.

'I'm afraid so, Mr Bligh,' she said. 'She is a gambler, a hussy who makes her living playing cards. The Devil has her soul!'

'The Devil he has!' said Bligh, vastly relieved that the woman had not turned to a far older profession, and they made their goodbyes and left.

'You seek her? Then we must try the gambling houses,' Chavez offered. He had obviously read Bligh's mind, and was making no attempt to disguise his amusement. Bligh returned his grin, and stepped instantly into the doorway of the Hatcher Saloon, surveyed the tables and was turning away when he heard a familiar giggle, followed by a deep-voiced oath and the clatter of an overturned chair. It came from a curtained alcove, and before he could stop himself, he pulled the curtain to one side.

Inside, four people were playing cards. Two were local businessmen, in shirt sleeves and sober vests, their jackets draped over the back of their chairs. The third man was on his feet, one hand on the table and the other reaching back for his hip.

He was a powerful man in shirt and jeans, with a fancy vest sadly worn and stained. Unlike the others, he wore boots and spurs, and his wide brimmed hat was hanging down his back by its chin strap. His hand of cards was spread out on the table alongside a pile of chips which was plainly his stake.

It was a good hand, with jacks and queens in it, but the hand which had beat it was spread out in front of Frankie Lewis and it contained kings. Many kings. The cowboy had taken a lot of drink, obviously did not like losing, and his dislike was about to turn into violence.

As he reached for his gun, one of the businessmen shouted, 'No! She won fair!' and grabbed for the cowboy's arm. The gun went off into the floor and Bligh stepped forward one long pace and smacked the barrel of his own pistol alongside the man's head. The gunman slumped forward over the table, and the table top tilted and poured all the stakes and cards onto the floor.

The shot had alerted the rest of the room to trouble brewing, and the patrons reacted according to their char-acters. Several reached for their own guns, more hit the floor face down, and a couple ran for the door.

Chavez was carrying his own rifle in his right hand, and he turned towards the room, with the weapon levelled.

Every man who could see him froze, some of them in the act of drawing their own weapons. The silence was thick enough to slice and serve with breakfast.

'Who is this trigger-happy clown?' asked Bligh, his pistol still in his hand. The clown rolled over and moaned feebly.

'He's a drover come in with the beef this morning,' replied the barman. 'Been drinking his wages all day, and I reckon you just saved his life. If he'd have hurt this lady here, they'd have strung him up from the hanging tree!'

'Lynched him?' said Chavez, slowly uncocking his rifle since the threat was over.

'Sure would. Good-looking women are a whole lot thinner on the ground hereabouts than hens' teeth,' said the barkeep. 'Set 'em up, boys! I reckon we owe these two *hombres* a drink!'

The drinks were duly set up, though Bligh noticed the barman paid for none of them and reckoned the cost had been absorbed by the wave of drinks bought by the barflies, and not by the management. He didn't mind. He needed a drink and despite his wages as gun guard and then driver on the coach, he was still sorely pressed.

Frankie closed down her poker game, taking the table stakes without even glancing at the cowboy, who was sitting up and looking muzzy, and the two businessmen made themselves scarce, leaving her and her rescuers. Two burly swampers dragged the semi-conscious cowboy outside and they heard splashing as they doused him with water from the horse trough.

Bligh sat down with Frankie, and Chavez put his rifle in the corner and joined them.

'I reckon you're some kind of female Jonah,' said Bligh,

settling himself comfortably to his whiskey and a cigar offered by a bystander with a bemused look.

'Jonah?' Frankie looked astonished. 'How in the name of all that's holy do you work that out? I had the winning hand!'

'But every time I see you, I have to get you out of some kind of trouble,' Bligh pointed out. 'What did you do for survival before you met me?'

Frankie grinned like a leprechaun. 'I got by, but I have to admit it's easier when I have a big man with a big gun to bail me out. What are you doing for the rest of my life?'

They all laughed, but Chavez shot Bligh a calculating look. Bligh caught it, and wondered.

'Truth to tell, I was hoping to run into you again, anyway,' said Frankie. 'I have something I wanted to talk about. There was something really funny about that hold up at Dragoon.'

Both men stared at her. Then Chavez said, 'You mean, there was something about it you did not understand? What?'

Frankie was playing with the deck of cards as she talked, dealing out dummy hands, face up, round the table. Bligh noticed that although she never dropped her eyes to look at her cards, she dealt herself three winning hands in succession. He began to wonder if the drunken cowboy had noticed something he shouldn't.

Frankie made two false starts before she said eventually, 'I reckon those hold up artists were looking for something, and didn't find it. They turned the place upside down even before they put us down in that glory hole.'

Chavez shrugged. 'Robbers rob, *señorita*. They look for things to steal. It is not very surprising, is it?'

She shook her head. 'It is not what I mean. First, they searched the stage office. There wasn't much there. A desk, a cupboard, a strong box where they kept the mail and some keys. I know that because it wasn't even locked. The bigger of the two men turned it out in front of us.'

The men waited.

'They searched us. Even the women. I thought the rancher was going to go for them, but Gilbourne held him back. Said it would not help his wife if he was dead. She told him to hold still, and put up with the search. It wasn't so bad. They really were looking for something, and they were mad when they couldn't find it, but there wasn't anything else. Nothing . . . ugly.'

Even so, it would go hard with the bandits when they were caught if it was known that they had mishandled a woman. Particularly a respectable one. Men had been lynched for less. The fact that they had been desperate enough to search the women indicated the bandits were desperate to find something.

He said as much, and Frankie nodded.

'Whatever it was, they didn't find it. When they had shut us into the cellar, they turned out our baggage. Did a thorough job, too. Ripped up anything bulky.'

Why anything bulky?

'Anything you could hide money in,' Frankie explained, gently. 'They were looking for money. Money or documents, and they didn't look much like lawyers to me.'

'And they didn't find it,' concluded Chavez. 'So—'

'So they planned to hit the stage again on the way into Tombstone,' finished Bligh, recalling his unease at the behaviour of the cactus wren. 'But a little bird told me to

66

be careful, and I was. So. . . .'

'So they will be here in town, waiting for a chance to search again for what they look for before,' Chavez finished. '*Señorita*, you are still in danger. And so are those nice Bedford folks.'

The Bedfords needed to be warned, and Frankie to be protected, and Bligh found to his surprise that he had no rooted objection to doing the protecting, though he suspected at the back of his mind that Frankie Lewis was about as vulnerable as a female timber wolf. She had not looked particularly worried when the drunken cowhand reached for his gun, and Bligh recalled that her right hand had been out of sight under the table during the whole episode.

The Bedfords, on the other hand, were both vulnerable and unsuspecting. He led the way back to the eating house, only to find they had finished their meal and gone.

'Where they staying? Hanged if I know,' reported the waiter at Nellie Cashmans's. 'Said it was close by and they sure as shooting would not be staying in the miners' cribs across the street. Try the Occidental; they got rooms, and so has the Grand.'

But the rancher and his wife had not got as far as the Grand. The barkeep directed them to the room all right, but it was empty. Their luggage had been tipped out over the bed, and ransacked. Linings had been ripped from their cases, and even the pillows and mattress gutted. Flock lay all over the floor.

Chavez exchanged a glance with Bligh, and all three of them ran down the stairs and into the street. Round the corner and into Fifth Street they went and were just starting down towards the restaurant again when they heard a muffled cry coming from between two buildings.

Tombstone was a network of alleyways and back lots between the buildings, it took three tries before they traced the source of the shouts. Mrs Bedford was lying against the wall in the dark of the alley, hands bound behind her and a pillow case, probably from their own room, pulled down over her head. Her husband was lying on his back further on, silent and still.

Bligh swore softly and left Mrs Bedford to Frankie, while he and Chavez reclaimed Bedford. To Bligh's deep relief, the man was still breathing, though unconscious, and they dragged him back into the street and under one of the lanterns. He had a nasty gash along the side of his head, and his face was bruised, but while they were moving him, he let out a deep groan and by the time they had him in the light, they could see his eyelids were flickering and he was trying to speak.

There was a doctor's office just along the block, and a light burned low in the upstairs window, so Chavez went and pounded on the door until he raised a roar of rage from within, and a bald man with bushes of white hair over his ears ripped open the door and waved an old cap-and-ball Colt, only slightly smaller than a field gun, under his nose.

The doctor put down his gun when he discovered this was a genuine emergency and opened his surgery to them. Mrs Bedford rolled up her sleeves and swabbed down her husband's face while the doctor fetched his bag, some rags and a pot of iodine.

'He's been roughed up some, and given a pistol whipping beside, but you can see most of the damage is on the outside, and there isn't anything vital broke,' opined the medical man when he had finished. 'Good night's sleep here and if his head's clear in the morning, he can go. Mrs Bedford can stay with him, but the rest of you people will have to find your own beds.

'I am open,' he said pointedly, 'from ten o'clock in the morning, and not until. Good night, lady and gents.' And he shut the door firmly in their faces.

CHAPTER SEVEN

Bedford admitted he was reputed to have a head made from a Rocky Mountain peak, but even so, his recovery seemed miraculous to Bligh when they took Art Knowles round to see him the following morning.

'Yeah, it was the same pair held us up at Dragoon,' he admitted, sitting up in the doctor's tiny two-bed hospital and sipping tea, which he referred to disgustedly as calves' water.

'One big man, he did the pistol whipping, and a smaller one, smelled of garlic. Mex, I reckon – beggin' your pardon and nothing personal,' he added, when he caught the hard glitter in Chavez' eyes.

'And they both had hoods on?' said Knowles, who was in charge this morning and would have much preferred the Earps to do their own investigations.

'Sure, but I'd know them again.'

'How?' said Knowles immediately. 'If you didn't see their faces and the best you can remember is that one is tall and one is short, and possibly a Mexican, how can you know them again? It was dark.'

The rancher leaned back on his pillows and pushed the tea away.

'That stuff is for a very sick calf,' he said. 'In the name of all that's holy, give me coffee.'

He shot a patient look at the deputy and held up a hand to count on his fingers.

'How would I know them again?' he said. 'One: I seen them before in full daylight and in the dusk. Two: the way they talk, the way they stand, the way they walk. Three: I smelled them, too. The little one eats garlic and chillies a lot. And I mean a *lot*! Four: I spend my life herding cows, mister. Cows may all look the same to you, with two horns at the front end, a leg at each corner, and no sense of responsibility at the back end, but they ain't. They're all different. Just like people.'

Chavez said, 'Cows are like people?'

'Yeah. Like people they all stand different; they all walk different; they all sound different; they even smell different. Ain't a calf in my herd I don't know. I know the quiet ones, and I know the ornery ones and, by Dad, I know the right mean ones that'll wait till your back's turned and then knock you down and trample you. And I know these two *hombres*. Man beats you about the head with a gun barrel, tends to make you remember him, and I remember these two like I was related to them .'

He put a hand to his head bandage and took it away again. 'By blood!' he added. 'That big man, he is right mean. Black-hearted, poison, nasty, mean.'

His wife was watching him with a mixture of worry and pride, and when the men stepped outside, she followed them.

'My Cole sure can talk when he gets his mad up,' she said with visible pride. 'But if he says he knows something, then by Glory, he knows it. You can count on that.'

71

Chavez grinned. 'He surely has his mad up now, *señora*, and he certainly can talk. There is more to it than what he said?'

She glanced uneasily up and down the street, already filling with people.

'Well, for one thing, that big man may be mean, but the little one, the Mexican? He's bad with women. I seen it before in a man and I sure know the signs.

'Tell you something else, too. He wasn't around in Tucson. The big one, yes. I seen him myself. He even had the same clothes on. That hood don't fool me none.'

She had little else to tell them, though she warned them not to mention the fact that she had recognized the big bandit.

'Neither of us would, ma'am,' Bligh reassured her. 'And best you don't tell your husband, neither. He's liable to go on the warpath, and these guys shape up to being real bad men. I think you been lucky, so far. Stay that way!'

They started to search Tombstone building by building and bar by bar, a huge task and one which was complicated by the fact that they had to look as though they were on a drinking spree, while actually consuming no liquor. Turning away Tombstone's cheapest rot-gut was no difficult task: it was said that it contained a rattlesnake head for strength and dead rats for body, and whether this was true or not, it certainly tasted like it.

But pouring the drink away and simulating growing drunkenness was a strain, and by mid afternoon, Chavez called a halt.

'I don't know about you, *amigo*, but I have poured so much cheap whiskey over my boots that I think they are rotting away. I need to eat, and I need to stop for a while.

72

If I cover this amount of ground, I need a horse and saddle.'

They stopped in at Nellie Cashman's and ate bacon and beans washed down with coffee, and when they had finished Bligh leaned back and rolled himself a cigarette.

'We're going about this the wrong way,' he said. 'Here we are looking in every saloon in the place, and he can just sit back and watch us knocking ourselves out. He knows where we are all the time, so he ain't coming out while we're walking the streets.'

Chavez gazed out of the window and nodded gloomily.

'You are right, of course. But if we stop searching, he can just get on his horse and ride away. We will not even know he has gone.'

Bligh leaned his elbows on the table, and nodded.

'But we are trying to find him, and what we need is for him to try and find us,' he said. 'What is he after?'

Chavez shrugged. 'Money.'

'Sure is. But what money? Passengers on the stage didn't have a lot. A girl gambler, looking for a new deck; a rancher and his wife – and them two ain't got no cash money to speak of. You can make a good living here ranching beef, but it's all in the ranch and the stock. You can't carry it on a stage, until you sell the herd. Like me.'

'That leaves Gilbourne, and he didn't seem to have a lot of cash money on him,' said Chavez thoughtfully.
'Contrariwise, he looks like money. Clothes were expensive, for the Territory. Boots were good, too. Handmade. And if he was robbed of much money, he didn't make much of a fuss about it. Which seems a strange thing for a man who likes to hear the sound of his own voice. Why not?'

He sat up in his chair suddenly.

'And where in tarnation is he?' he said. 'We been in darned near every saloon and drinking hole in town today, and I ain't seen hide, hair nor tallow of the man. He said something suggested to me that he had a business in Tombstone. So where is it? Ain't seen no sign anyplace saying Gilbourne Enterprises, have you?'

Chavez shook his head.

Bligh called the waitress, and asked her if she knew a Gilbourne Enterprises office. She shook her head dubiously.

'I never heard the name,' she said. 'And Tombstone isn't that big. If it was here, I'd know. You tried asking at the marshal's office?'

They had not, but they paid their tab and went straight there. Knowles looked at them sourly.

'No, I ain't heard of a Gilbourne Enterprises,' he said. 'Nor yet a Gilbourne ranch. Nor a Gilbourne office, nor a Gilbourne store, nor a Gilbourne saloon. Who is Gilbourne, when he's to home? Passenger on the stage? Then maybe he was passing through.'

Back on the street, Bligh remembered the girl gambler and was surprised to find he was looking forward to finding her again. Characteristically, she was sitting behind a table covered in cards and money, and showing a good deal more cleavage than she had the last time he saw her.

'Hello there, Bligh!' she called when she saw him. 'I've been looking for you. Give me time to finish this hand, and you can buy me a drink.'

One of the players, a professional gambler by his looks, folded his hand and pocketed his stake money.

'Finish it now, for all of me, lady,' he said glumly.

'Luck's another lady ain't with me today.'

The other two players stayed in and lost when she showed her hand, but they stood up with good enough grace.

'You be around tonight, Miz Lewis?' said one, as he shrugged on his coat. 'I can try and get some of my money back, if you are.'

She smiled warmly enough. 'Sure, I'll be here, Harry,' she said. 'Bring your lucky boots with you this time though. These ones don't seem to be doing you any favours a-tall!'

They went off cheerfully enough, a remarkable result when the dealer had seen most of the game and, as they went, she shrugged a shawl over her shoulders and knotted it.

'I need to talk to you anyway, Bligh,' she said, when he raised his eyebrows. 'And I want your mind entirely on business today. Sit down.' She waved at the bar and the barkeep, a thin, balding man with a moustache like a walrus, brought her a tray with a bottle and three glasses. The whiskey was surprisingly good, and Bligh said so.

'Local brew's only good for embalming miners,' Frankie said with a wink. 'But that doesn't mean you can't get anything better, if you ask the right man. Harry's the right man, aren't you, Harry?'

The thin man gave a surprisingly bright grin, and nodded as he went back to the bar.

Frankie poured more drink, and leaned on the table.

'Have you seen Gilbourne since we got here?' she asked. Bligh and Chavez, suddenly all attention, leaned closer.

'You haven't? Want to know where he is?'

She looked like a woman with a secret, so Bligh asked her what it was.

'He's taken a whole suite at the Cattleman's Rest,' she said. 'And tonight, I am dining with him. In his suite. Alone.'

Bligh found to his amazement that he did not like the idea one little bit. He told himself it was ridiculous to resent it when a businessman asked a pretty girl to dinner, particularly a girl who made her living in a saloon, playing cards.

But he still didn't like the idea and she knew it and grinned more widely.

'What's the matter, Tom?' she said. 'Worried about my modesty?'

He had his mouth open to deny it hotly, but she laid her hand on his and silenced him.

'Sweet of you, honey,' she said. 'But I am quite capable of taking care of myself. I have been doing it for more years than I care to admit to, and I'm no schoolgirl.

'But doesn't it strike you as being odd that brother Manfred was the only one of us not particularly upset at being robbed in the coach-station hold-up? His clothes are expensive, and his baggage is hand stitched. His boots cost more than all my clothes put together, valise included.'

Chavez nodded. Bligh had to admit that when he thought about it, Gilbourne had not been particularly upset at being held up, robbed and locked in a cellar. While the other passengers had been complaining about their looted baggage, Gilbourne had been silent.

'Suppose, just suppose, that the hold up men were not after our money really, but something else?'

'What else?'

'Well. Suppose the loot from El Mexicano's previous raids was supposed to be on that coach – but they couldn't find it? He got it out of Tucson somehow, and from what you told me, he didn't have time between you seeing him in the saloon and holding up the blacksmith to do much else with it. Suppose he had already consigned it to the coach line, and the only way he could get it back was to steal it?

'That coach had been gone through pretty brutally up at the Dragoon Station. Seats ripped up, some panels kicked in. All our baggage was opened and the lining was cut on my valise at any rate.'

'So?'

'What were they after? Not the few bits of jewellery I have, certainly. They ignored most of it. Not Mrs Bedford's pretty beads – did you know they were real pearls? They are, and they would have bought that coach twice over.'

'What, then?'

'Money. Paper money, gold, or documents. Any idea how much a mining concession in Tombstone would be worth? Ed Schieffelin might have made himself a millionaire when he found the silver here, but he sold out. But the rights on a good silver deposit would make him look like a pauper.'

Bligh could see her point, though so far as he was concerned, all he wanted was the money for his cattle and a long ride home. He had seen Ed, the discoverer of Tombstone, sleeping it off more than once, and he didn't look like the town owner – he looked like the town drunk.

So if the loot El Mexicano and his sidekick were after was not in the coach, and it had not been in the passengers' luggage, where could it be?

Dragoon Station was the only place it could possibly have been. The passengers had not been out of his or Chavez' sight at any time since they had been released from the cellar. Assuming the loot had not been taken by the Pima boy or the station agent, it had to be still there, somewhere.

And El Mexicano and his partner were not be found around town. He shot a glance at Chavez and he could see that the Mexican officer had come to the same conclusion he had.

They were looking in the wrong place.

CHAPTER EIGHT

When they finally got the clerk at the Cattleman's Rest to let them into Gilbourne's suite, they realized just how badly they had judged their prey.

The table was set for dinner, and dinner had clearly been eaten. There was even a half empty champagne bottle in the tepid water which was all that remained of the ice in the ice bucket. The remains of the meal were still on the plates, and one whole champagne glass and a mess of broken glass which had been the other were among the remains on the table.

Of Frankie and Gilbourne himself, there was no sign.

'Mr Gilbourne and his guest went out around midnight,' the clerk told them through lips compressed like a prune. 'He called for a buckboard to be brought, and we got one round from the stables in ten minutes. Don't like to be kept waiting, Mr Gilbourne.'

Chavez restrained Bligh from dragging the man across the reception desk, and asked in a reasonable voice, 'Did they say where they were going?'

The clerk got a foxy look about the eyes and started hemming and hawing. This time, Chavez lost his temper, and before Bligh could do anything, he had the man pinned against the key rack.

'*Hombre*,' said the Mexican in a soft voice. 'Look down, but be careful not to make any sudden moves.'

The clerk looked down and found seven inches of razor-sharp steel poised just below his belt buckle. The point of the knife had penetrated his clothing and was just stinging the soft flesh of his belly. He swallowed noisily.

'Now, I ask again. There is, you will understand, a certain urgency about the situation,' Chavez said in his silkiest voice. 'And I am not a patient man. You are ready?'

The clerk gulped and nodded. His eyes were agonized.

'Where did they go?'

The breath whistled in the man's throat. But with the steel at his gut, he found his voice.

'He said they were going out to look at the moon,' he said. 'But just after he left, I heard French Belle's dogs barking. She lives up to the east end of Fremont. I reckon they made for the north road. Maybe for the Dragoons.'

Chavez nodded. 'Anything else?'

'Yeah,' said the clerk in whose imagination Chavez' blade was almost grating on his backbone, 'Two other horses left town about an hour later. Belle's dogs barked then, too.'

Chavez pushed his knife back into his boot, and let go of the man's throat. The unfortunate clerk, unsupported, slid down the wall like a handful of wet spaghetti.

'*Adios, hombre*,' Chavez said in a friendly voice. 'We go now. If I find that you have been lying to me, I promise you we will be back and we will not be happy. Neither will you.'

He flashed a dazzling smile, and the two men shouldered out of the doors and made for their horses.

'Everything seems to hinge on the Dragoon Station,'

Bligh said, as they saddled up. 'I reckon we make for there. The buggy tracks should be easy enough to find in the dust; there ain't much traffic up that way, recent.'

In the event, Bligh and Chavez could see the dust in front of them as they climbed into the mountains towards Dragoon Station.

But midday came and went without their managing to catch up, and it became obvious that they were not going to catch it before it got to the stage station.

They stopped at a small tank off the trail to water themselves and their horses.

'At first,' Chavez said, 'I thought he was going to the station. Now I think not. I think he goes beyond the station, and El Mexicano will follow him because El Mexicano thinks he knows where there is treasure.'

Bligh thought the same and said so.

'If we are following the big man and the gambling lady,' he said, 'where is El Mexicano? He must be just as interested in them as we are. He could be between us and them.'

'You're missing out a possibility,' Bligh argued. 'That maybe it is El Mexicano and his sidekick we are following, and if it is, maybe they can see Gilbourne ahead of them the same distance they are ahead of us.'

Chavez nodded and hunkered down carefully. He was wearing Mexican spurs with big spiked rowels, and the wise man allowed space for them.

'Certainly we do not catch up with them, whoever they may be,' he said. 'In this country, maybe that just shows they are wise men. But most travellers are curious about who follows them, and by this time they must realize we are on their trail.'

They mounted up. The dust cloud had moved further away, but it was definitely making for the Dragoon Springs Station, and the two men pulled off the trail, and began threading their way through the rocks which fringed the foot of the Dragoons.

It was hard, awkward going. The rocks here were stacked like giant building blocks, sometimes in crazy shapes. The Apaches had often led Crook's cavalry a merry chase in this labyrinth, and Bligh knew his way through them only because he had so often searched them for missing stock.

'We'll water the horses at the station,' he told Chavez, when the Mexican mentioned the subject.

Chavez followed him through a gap in the rampart, where the rock folded back on itself concealing the way through to anybody who did not already know of it. At the top, Bligh was waiting, standing in his stirrups and staring through his field glasses.

'We're ahead of them,' he said. 'Station's just over that ridge, and I can see the dust beyond it. We can beat them to it.'

He led off, and the men cantered down the side of the near ridge and climbed the far one to find themselves overlooking the stage road as it approached the station. The source of the dust was not yet in sight, but they could see the vague mistiness over the brow of the trail where it came over the shoulder of the hill, so it was still on the road.

They clattered up to the station to find the gates closed, and when they hammered on them, Maria Wilson's head appeared over the wall accompanied by the barrels of a shotgun and she shouted shrilly, '*Quien es?*'

Bligh hastily identified them. Maria Wilson often did the shooting for the pot at the station, and her aim was deadly. So was her habit of using buckshot on almost anything bigger than a quail. She stared down at them and Bligh took off his hat to show his face.

'*Buenas tardes, señora!*' Chavez shouted, and Maria grinned, told them to wait a moment, and disappeared. One of the gates opened with a clatter, though only wide enough to allow the horses through, and she slammed it shut behind them.

Inside, the place had changed, There were shutters with loopholes cut into them over the windows which faced the yard, and at the sound of the gate being opened, Harry Wilson appeared in the doorway to the living quarters. He also had a shotgun in his hand, and both hammers were cocked.

'You point that there scattergun someplace else, Harry,' Bligh told him sharply. 'We got enough problems without buckshot round our ears. There's folks coming we want to head off here.'

The station agent let down the hammers on his gun and walked out into the yard. From the stables, the Pima boy emerged, a pitchfork in his hand, but when he recognized the newcomers, he put it down and nodded at them gravely. On him, it was the equivalent of three cheers and a round of applause, and Bligh waved at him.

'Sorry about the gun. We heard two shots not too far away a half-hour back. Wasn't you, was it? Who you meeting here?' Wilson asked.

'No, we ain't fired no shots, so it wasn't us. As for who we're meeting, there's a buggy coming up the road from Tombstone. If it's got Gilbourne and Miss Lewis in it, we guessed right. If it hasn't, we need to find them, and fast.'

Wilson crossed the compound in a few quick steps, ran up the ladder to the firing platform over the gate and produced a telescope which looked as though John Paul Jones had left it last time he sailed by. Wilson leaned it on the rampart over the gate, and stared down the road.

'Ain't no sign of it from here, and there should be, if they're within a half-hour or so,' he said. 'You can see a good way down the road, that's why they built here. If your guess was right, maybe they got intercepted.'

'Fooled, by damn!' Bligh swore.

Wilson shook his head. 'Where else would they be going?' he asked. 'This is the best stop between here and the San Pedro. Go further west and you need water bad.'

He checked through the telescope, and shrugged. 'That rider you mentioned? No sign of him, neither. Think they went someplace together?'

Bligh did think they went someplace else. By this time he was convinced that the three people he was seeking were the three who had been on the road – Frankie Lewis, Gilbourne and El Mexicano.

He was haunted, too, by the thought that Frankie might not have been abducted by Gilbourne, but be an accomplice of the man. They had been riding the same stage, after all. Been held up and imprisoned by the same man. And she seemed to have gone off to dinner with the man without a second thought, even in Tombstone where true civilization was said to be two rivers and a state away.

Could the man have abducted her from the middle of Tombstone without anybody noticing? It seemed a very remote possibility, and now she was out in the rugged mountain country with the man.

And El Mexicano.

He ran down the ladder, and hoisted himself into the saddle without bothering about his stirrups. Chavez was hardly a pace behind him.

'I think maybe your lady friend could be in trouble, *amigo!*' he shouted. 'Big, bad trouble!'

So did Bligh, and the two men went down the slope to the road at a flat gallop. There was, amazingly, no dust trail to follow now. Both the buggy and the pursuing rider had disappeared without leaving a trace.

The only explanation was that the buggy and the rider had both continued along the main road towards the north, instead of swinging off it to the stage station. They hit the road at a flat gallop, then pulled to a standstill while they searched the ground for tracks.

It seemed hopeless. The road was well used and the surface full of tracks, one overlaying the other. The broad tyres of the stage were easy enough to pick out, wide and smooth like ribbons in the dust. The hoofprints were impossible.

'Me, I did not think there had been this many riders in a year,' swore Chavez, leaning down almost to his horse's knees to examine a particularly clear set. 'Maybe this could be made this morning, maybe last week. It is clear, but not too clear.'

Bligh straightened up from his hunkered-down position and stared around over the surrounding land.

'No tracks we can get a hold on. No sign of the buggy or the horse. No dust,' he growled. 'How in tarnation do we find them? Yet they got to be round here, someplace. Nowhere else to go!'

Chavez climbed out of his stirrups and stood on his

saddle, to give himself a greater range of sight, then searched the land with the field-glasses. After a minute or so, he shook his head, dropped into the saddle again and shrugged. On Chavez a shrug said as much as a political speech.

'*Nada*,' he said disgustedly. 'I can see nothing. No tracks, no buggy, no rider. Not even any dust. . . .'

Their eyes met, and both men swore luridly.

'No dust, then maybe they ain't moving,' said Bligh bitterly. 'If they ain't moving, they stayed where they were. They're not at the station and they are not on the road, so they're someplace between here and the point where the road goes behind the big rock on the bluff. Come on!'

They turned back down the road and rode, one either side of the track, searching carefully. There was no way of telling the difference between El Mexicano's horse – assuming it was he following the buggy – and any other traveller.

But there had only been one buggy on the road that morning, and there was no way of disguising its tyre tracks. Those iron hoops would leave traces like ribbons where the vehicle had left the road.

And so they had.

Chavez suddenly stopped his horse and leaned down from the saddle, then whistled to attract Bligh's attention.

When the rancher rode over, Chavez pointed at the ground without getting off his horse.

'It is here,' he said. 'They go south.'

At this point below the stage station, and out of sight of its gates, the ground was firm and dry. There was a scattering of sere grasses along the foot of the bluff itself, but little other vegetation apart from the eternal dusty green of the ocotillo cacti and the reaching arms of the saguaro.

Bligh reined in and stared down the line of the wheel tracks. The trail led downhill before swinging in behind yet another pile of boulders. He was about to ride down and follow it when his natural caution exerted itself.

If there was no dust, then the buggy and its pursuer could have stopped moving. The only place they could have stopped and been out of sight was that same pile of rocks, so unless they had developed the power of flight, their quarry had to be in or behind that rockpile.

If they were, as he suspected, after the loot El Mexicano had lost from the coach, then they could not be far from the road. Assuming the loot had been hidden, it must have been hidden by one of the passengers, and they had not had time to get very far from the coach.

Indeed, now he thought about it, he could not understand how whoever had hidden the loot had time to get down to this point on the road. There was no reason for the coach to stop here, for one thing. How could a stage passenger have got down for long enough to hide what must be a valuable parcel? He or she could hardly ask the coach driver to wait awhile so they could dig a hole and bury it.

Cautiously, they rode forward round the side of the rocks, following the faint buggy tracks, until they were on the southern edge of it.

The buggy was there, all right, standing in plain sight, though the horse was missing. Under it lay a body, face down and packed into the shade of the vehicle, where it would not attract the attention of the turkey buzzards.

Chavez dismounted quietly and walked to the vehicle, being careful not to disturb tracks, though he need not have bothered. The ground here was rough and stony, with a few ocotillo and greasewood plants scattered in it. There was no cover to hide an ambusher, and no obvious tracks.

He turned the body onto its back. The dead man was a Mexican, dressed in a serape and trousers, his sombrero was stuffed under the wagon with him. He had been shot twice in the back. His pistol was still in its holster.

Bligh stood and cast around, working his way back to the edge of the bluff, until he suddenly found horse tracks, and froze.

Chavez was examining the ground and did not look up before he called out, 'Nothing here, *amigo*. Anything your way?'

'Sure is. Come see,' called Bligh, and the Mexican walked his horse up the slopes. Bligh pointed at the ground, where horse tacks could easily be seen.

'More than one animal. If they're trying not to be traced, they sure ain't trying terrible hard,' he said. 'Ground's hard and dry, though. Not much dust to leave a trace. How many do you make it?'

Chavez knelt and looked closely. There were droppings by the tracks and he poked them apart with a stick.

'At least three,' he said finally. 'About half an hour. The droppings, they are fresh. Looks like our people, and they knew where they want to go!'

Together, they rode in the tracks, occasionally losing them on the hard ground. Chavez was as good a tracker as an Indian, and he always picked them up again, but their progress was slow.

'They follow the line of the road,' said Chavez after a while. 'Not on it, but with it. Where do they go?'

Bligh grinned a tight, hard grin. 'Follow the line and it leads to gold,' he said. 'That murdering sidewinder is after his loot, and either the girl or that fancy pants Gilbourne knows where it is. That's why he's got them with him. Now I reckon I know why that other renegade was shot. He was riding the spare horse.'

Chavez looked grave.

'If you are right, then we had better hurry. If he does not hesitate to kill his partner for a horse, he will not mind shooting a witness for his safety. And by now, both of those people may have seen enough of him to recognize him again.'

In the closing dusk, they rode on together following the road.

CHAPTER NINE

Frankie Lewis sat awkwardly propped on the back of the dead bandit's horse, one knee hooked around the saddle horn, as though she were riding side saddle. Since the saddle was a Mexican one, with a high cantle and broad, elaborate horn, this put her in an uncomfortable, insecure position.

Twice, the one they called El Mexicano glared at her and told her gruffly to ride astride, and twice she shot him a withering glance and told him she was a lady and ladies did not ride that way. She even managed a deep blush on the second occasion, and cast her eyes down modestly.

Gilbourne sniggered when she said it, and she marked him down for the first shot out of the pistol she was concealing under her skirts.

But the gun harness she had designed herself had been knocked awry when she was struggling with Gilbourne in the buggy earlier on, and the pistol was now jammed on the front of her thigh. She could not easily reach it without alerting both men to what she was doing. And if she tried to ride astride, the pistol would be outlined against the tight drawn material.

The men might not realize what it was at first, but they

would certainly guess if she tried to pull up her skirts and grope for the gun between her legs. The aperture she had let into the seam on the outside of her left thigh, to let her draw the weapon without raising her skirts, was now far from the holster and useless.

If push came to shove, she told herself, she would hoick up her skirts to the waist, and grab for the gun. With any luck, and supposing she did not get caught up in the folds of her own underwear, she could get at least one of them and, if she timed it right, she might even get both.

For the umpteenth time, she cursed her own stupidity in entrusting herself to Gilbourne and the hidden gun. She had only done it because Tom Bligh seemed so cocky about wanting to take care of her. She prided herself on her ability to look after herself without depending on a man.

Tom Bligh. She shifted uncomfortably in the saddle again and wondered where he was. From the moment Gilbourne had knocked the champagne glass out of her hand halfway through their dinner and twisted her arm behind her back, she had been wondering that.

It had seemed such a simple proposition to start with. Gilbourne seemed no different from any of the men who sat themselves down across her card table and set out to go broke by underestimating her and overestimating their own card playing skill. It had happened so often, she had come to be amused at their stupidity.

Gilbourne, however, was not stupid and certainly was not to be distracted by her low cut gown, however often she leaned forward over the table. The eyes which noted the gesture were spitefully amused by it, but not fooled.

And she had been stupid. She acknowledged that to

herself, bitterly.

She had judged Gilbourne to be just another self satisfied adventurer come to cash in on Tombstone's riches.
For the town was rich – fabulously rich, and as open as the
desert itself.

The riches under the very streets of the town named
after a soldier's joke were only just being realized. When a
worn-down prospector called Ed Schieffelin set out from
Fort Huachuca towards the Dragoons, a wiseacre soldier
told him, 'All you'll find there will be your tombstone.'

Schieffelin, grinning from ear to ear, christened his first
strikes Graveyard and Tombstone. Huachuca never let the
soldier forget it – and just to rub it in, the miners called
the town Tombstone as well.

Naturally, it attracted trouble, and the trouble attracted
men like Manfred Gilbourne.

Other thieves might lust after the silver which flowed
out of the ground but Gilbourne lusted after the land
itself. And he had come to Tombstone to get it.

To get a foothold in that land, he needed money, and
to get the money, he needed a thief. To a man from the
East, El Mexicano might have looked just the man he
needed. He was ruthless, clever, brave and capable. He was
also intelligent, and when he had worked out why
Gilbourne needed him, he decided to make himself more
than just the muscle in the partnership.

His raids on the stage lines – and on the railroad, the
banks and the gold mining shipments, when he felt like it
– brought in the money all right, but he was not, unlike so
many other robbers, stealing money merely to squander it
on drunken sprees and women: El Mexicano wanted
riches, and he meant to keep what he stole.

He stole a lot. Stage passengers by definition had money, and many of them brought with them into the West riches to invest and make profits. Railroad passengers carried their jewellery, as well as money and often bonds to invest in the new territories.

El Mexicano raided the wagons when he found them broken away from the main wagon trains, but they were usually poor pickings. People who had to walk across a continent instead of riding the rails or sailing round the Horn were not people loaded with riches.

But he had done well from the miners carrying their pokes in soft leather pouches, and cattlemen taking their profits home with them. The haul from the east-bound coach coming down from Maricopa Wells had been a particularly good one.

He swore to himself when he remembered how his carefully laid plans had fallen apart at that point. The hold-up of the Tucson bound coach had seemed such a push-over. All he had to do was stop it, grab the valuables and make for his hideout – but it started to go wrong right away.

First the damned guard had tried for his shotgun, and El Mexicano had to shoot him. Then the cattleman had produced a gun from somewhere and opened fire. From the tiny popping of the little pistol, it was a hideout gun, but even a .22 slug at close range could kill. One had sliced his arm in passing.

Then he had been forced to go back to Maricopa Wells after the hold-up to collect his loot and that in turn involved stashing his horse and the easily identifiable weapons and hood because the passengers on the stage would have recognized them immediately.

The idea of sending his loot out of town in the very stage-line he had robbed had seemed like a stroke of genius at the time. His partner, Gilbourne, the business-man who kept him supplied with information, would have had to keep quiet during the hold-up and watch him ride away with all their ill-gotten gains, and been unable to do anything at all about it.

Instead, the accursed cow-rancher, now unexpectedly riding guard, had cut loose with the shotgun and nobody in his right mind stayed to argue with buckshot. This man, unlike the first guard, had been loaded, ready and shot without a second's thought.

It had not been hard to recruit a sidekick in the person of the Mexican, Sanchez. The man would have sold his sister for the price of a drink, and his character made it all the easier for El Mexicano to kill him simply to take his horse.

It was the damned rancher who dogged him like an evil spirit. First the hold-out gun, then the shotgun at the second hold-up; the relentless pursuit – where in the name of all that was holy had he managed to recruit the Mexican partner? – and the cursed chance meeting in Tucson. There was no question that he had been recog-nized, and once again, the cow-chaser had been quick off the mark, and nearly had him.

But the disappearance of his loot from the stagecoach's strongbox was just another final disaster in the catalogue of disasters. It was not on the stage, nor in the passengers' luggage. When he had got to Tombstone, he was equally certain that Gilbourne didn't have it, so that left only the rancher and his wife, and the girl.

But when he had been seen in Tucson, the startled look

he got from the damned cattleman in the saloon told him he had also been recognized. He had managed to extricate himself from there neatly enough, but he knew that the wounded paint horse he had been riding at the hold-up would identify him immediately.

He had ridden it until it was ready to drop, and then shot it and abandoned the carcass in the water-hole, where it would be most inconvenient to his pursuer.

He was aware that the cattleman he had robbed and who was hunting him down had somehow acquired a Mexican companion though he was unaware of that Mexican's true identity. He knew, solely, that together they were like a pair of hounds baying on his trail, and he knew it was time to break away and make for his hideaway among the little towns and haciendas of northern Mexico.

But he would not leave without his money, and that money had gone missing.

He shot another glance at the woman, and wondered once again why she insisted on riding in that ridiculous and obviously uncomfortable position when riding astride would be both more comfortable and more stable.

The girl was an unnecessary complication, and he had already decided that when they had recovered the money, he would shoot her. A pity, really, she was a handsome woman, and had a fine figure – but she was also a woman with a strong personality and he knew that if he took her with him, he would never sleep sound at night.

Sooner or later, she would get to him, and she looked like a woman with an inventive turn of mind. No, better dead, he decided, though the thought of what he would do to her first made him smile to himself.

Frankie Lewis saw that smile, and her stomach

contracted. She would have to be absolutely certain to kill him first and if necessary take her chances with Gilbourne, she thought. She wished, for the umpteenth time, that she had managed to get the pistol into a better position.

Gilbourne watched the interplay between the two, and filed it away in his mind. He worked better when the opposition was divided against itself, and so far as Gilbourne was concerned, the entire world was the opposition.

The matter of the robber's loot was a distraction from his main purpose, though essential to it, and he resented it. He needed that money to start his assault on the riches of Tombstone, and that did not mean he needed half of it: it meant he needed it all.

His personal preference would have been to build a slow fire and hold the little tart's feet over it until she screamed the location of the loot. He was certain she knew, because he was certain she had taken it. He could even work out where she had taken it – at one of the comfort stops on the route down from Tucson.

He knew El Mexicano was convinced that the money had been on the coach when it pulled into the Dragoon Springs Station, and that the outlaw had planned to take it there. Gilbourne had known nothing about the Mexican bandit El Mexicano had recruited until he had seen them together in Tombstone and by then his plans to kidnap Frankie Lewis were already set, and he was in no position to argue.

Even he had been mildly shocked by El Mexicano's murder of the Mexican. The outlaw had done it with as little emotion as if he were discussing the change in share prices on the New York exchange, or the prospect of rain in the Tombstone area during the coming monsoon moths.

'Him?' he had replied, when Gilbourne asked about the Mexican. 'We needed an extra horse, so I took his. There was no way he would have overlooked it, we would have had him on our trail forever. So I shot him.'

So far as El Mexicano was concerned, that was explanation enough. It also served as a warning to Gilbourne that murder was not a major issue in the bandit's mind.

'Why do you call yourself El Mexicano?' he asked the man, idly. 'You aren't Mexican, and you don't look it.'

'So they aren't looking for an Anglo,' said the bandit. 'In town, I'm just another wandering cowhand who shows up now and again and keeps his own company.'

'In towns? I can't see why you need to go into towns.'

The look he shot Gilbourne would have warned the man he was on dangerous ground, if he had been looking. But he was not, and missed a chance to draw back.

'When we find the money,' Gilbourne said, 'I'll take it into town and bank it. That'll make it respectable. Then I can draw out your half and you can do what you like with it. I've some business plans for my half, and if you want to come in with me, I am perfectly happy to row you in on the deal. It will probably make more money than whatever you are planning for it.'

He turned the horse away and rode it up the slope and on to the road so, once again, he missed the change of expression in the bandit's eyes when he volunteered to invest the money. It would have told him much and warned him more.

But all thoughts of betrayal went out of his mind when they turned the corner in the trail and looked down on the silver streak fringed by trees in the distance which was the San Pedro. The comfort stop for the coaches was immediately in front of them, marked by a stand of cotton-wood trees. There was no building there or staff, merely a grove of cottonwoods where travellers could stretch their legs, and a crude flat roof on legs. There was a well but it was intermittent and this was plainly not its wet season.

'Down there.' Gilbourne pointed and El Mexicano nodded and urged his horse onwards, picking up the pace, slightly. The increased speed raised the dust from the trail and left a plume behind them.

Gilbourne urged his horse forward until he was riding knee to knee with the woman, and leaned towards her.

'Time for a talk, my dear,' he said. 'Since my colleague down there in front is a practical man, I would advise you to tell him where you hid that valise of mine you took from the stage last time we were here. Otherwise, the rest of your life is likely to be brief and brutal and filled with pain.

'He is not a patient man, though I am told he is painstaking. Tell him what he wants to know, and I swear I will protect you from him.'

For the first time, she was genuinely frightened. Nobody knew she was out here with these men. There was nobody within miles to hear her if she screamed and from the expression on Gilbourne's face, she would most certainly be screaming.

On the other hand, the only thing which was keeping her alive at the moment, she was convinced, was the fact that she knew where their money was hidden. Once she had given up that secret, she would also be giving up her life, so it was a case of keeping her mouth tight shut, and hoping to convince them that she did know where the money was, but was not to be forced into telling them.

She swallowed hard, and wondered if she could get her hand on her gun before they grabbed her.

'What makes you think—?' she started, but the bandit swore suddenly, and both of them looked at him. He was staring back along the face of the hill down which they had just come.

'What?' said Gilbourne. A pistol had appeared in his hand as though it had grown there suddenly. It was rock steady, and he held it more professionally than any businessman should.

Even from a few miles back, Bligh and Chavez saw the dust and increased their pace. Bligh remembered the grove of trees and the spring with its low wall of dry stones, so he knew where the men were taking the girl.

In front of him the road climbed, and then, he remembered, swooped down to the grove, and he expected to see the horses tethered there, by the well. He took his field glasses and focused on the group.

At first, he thought they had somehow detected his presence, and ducked back. Then he realized they had been looking up the slope, but not directly in his direction. Something else had attracted their attention.

He backed from the crest and swept the length of the low ridge with his field-glasses. Almost instantly, to the south, he picked up the haze of dust which had also been seen by their quarry. It was too big to indicate a single horseman, or even a couple. That cloud of dust was big enough to mean a group.

Or a patrol – and almost as he worked it out, he could

see the dark shapes emerging from a small arroyo and making for the spring.

'Blue bellies!' he said to himself, and Chavez snapped an amused glance in his direction.

'Blue what?' he said.

'Blue bellies – horse soldiers,' Bligh told him. 'A patrol. They must be out making sure all the Indians are coming back to the reservation. Maybe combing for renegades, though there ain't been no raids I know of. Them warriors passed us the other morning could have cut down on us, and didn't.'

'So why the soldiers?'

Bligh shrugged. 'You get renegade Apaches just like you get renegade Yankees,' he said. 'You get them down below the Border just like we get them up here.'

The soldiers, though, didn't seem to be moving with any urgency. They rode down to the grove relaxed and casual, like men looking forward to coffee and a rest in the shade.

To Bligh's surprise, Gilbourne walked out to meet them with one hand held up, palm outwards. The officer pulled his men to a standstill outside the grove and rode forward to talk to him. His men reined in on command, and eased themselves in the saddle while the talk went on.

Down in the trees, El Mexicano knelt by Frankie Lewis with his knife pressed into her neck. He was holding her down on a spread blanket with one hand twisted behind her back and his knee held her feet immobile on the ground. From a few yards away with his knife concealed by his body, he looked like a solicitous husband tending a sick wife, and that was precisely what the young lieutenant in command of the patrol saw.

'We think it could be typhoid, Lieutenant,' Gilbourne was saying in a deep and serious voice. 'She's been ailing for a couple of days, and we were taking her by buckboard to Tucson, but the buggy broke an axle back a-ways, and she rode until she was too sick to ride any longer.'

The lieutenant was not a fool, but neither did he know exactly what to do with a sick woman out in the desert. What he did know was that typhoid could go through a town like a savage horde, killing where it touched. He had seen Western towns left depopulated by a bad outbreak, and he had no desire to see another.

'Who is she?' he asked. He was trying to stay upwind of Gilbourne and his companions without being obvious about it, and not making a very good job.

Gilbourne noted his nerves and decided to push his luck.

'Care to do me a favour, Lieutenant?' he said, edging forward to make the officer edge back and further away from the girl and the bandit.

'What?'

'When you get to the fort, could you ask the medical officer to come out and look at her? I don't want to take her too close to the town until we know just what kind of typhoid she's got. Could be very dangerous. This one develops quickly – she was fine two days ago, and now. . . . Well, you see how it is.'

The lieutenant could indeed see the writhing figure on the blankets and hear from time to time a muted cry like an animal in pain, and he wanted no part of it. The soldiers, who had heard the word 'typhoid', were already restive.

'Medical officer? We certainly will, mister,' he said. He mounted, turned the horse on a dime and scurried back to his command. An order, and they started away from the well and back to the road.

CHAPTER TEN

'Damn them to Satan and all his demons!' Bligh exploded, as he saw the cavalry riding away from the cottonwood grove. He had expected the soldiers to settle down to make their coffee and effectively anchor the two men with their female captive in place.

That achieved, he and Chavez could ride up and gently extract her and make off. El Mexicano and Gilbourne would have been powerless to stop them. Instead, he had to watch their salvation ride away, too far away to shout at, and moving too fast to catch up in a short time.

In the tense atmosphere of the settling of the Indian troubles, a shot might start a pitched battle before all parties knew what was going on. A prolonged pursuit was out of the question. By the time they had caught up with the cavalry and had convinced the officer to return with them, the two men would have been well away with their hostage, and what they might do to her in the meantime did not bear thinking about.

'I think they are breaking camp, *amigo*,' Chavez said suddenly, and he looked back towards the grove to see the men hustling the girl on to her horse and mounting up themselves. They were plainly not taking any chances on the cavalry returning, or on being interrupted by anybody else.

'Will they be caught by the coach coming through?' the Mexican asked him, staring at the camp. He had no field glasses, and Bligh passed over his own. Chavez could leave the coach out of his calculations, though. The morning coach would have gone on its way east, and the evening one was not due through to the west for hours.

They mounted up hurriedly, and keeping the ridge between them and their quarry, followed along as the men took their captive north.

'If we just ride up and try to take her, they'll kill her, sure as shooting,' Bligh said, when Chavez suggested the idea. Chavez privately agreed with him, but his purpose was to catch and kill the outlaw, not to rescue the girl, however desirable that might be. Frankie Lewis was decorative and bright, but she was not, strictly, his concern. His duty was the kill the bandit and get back to his own side of the border before the authorities knew he had crossed into their territory.

The two men followed the fugitives and the girl as they wound their way up into the hills to the north of the river crossing. Up here, the ground was broken and massive boulders bigger than houses piled one on top of the other making a maze of tiny trails and tunnels.

'They ain't going to get to any settlement before dark,' he told the Mexican uneasily as the journey stretched towards the night. Up in the mountains there were small towns and mining camps, but the men could hardly take their hostage into anywhere she might call for help.

In any case, he reminded himself uncomfortably, the men would need secrecy for what they wanted to do, and even the most rough hewn Westerner would be enraged at the deliberate mistreatment of a woman. He had heard of one man being burned to death for rape.

But the pair of outlaws seemed to be moving with purpose and not merely scouting around for some convenient spot for the night. Their trail clung to a settled direction, and they ignored what looked like several equally promising side trails.

By this time, the girl had changed her riding position, and was riding like a man. When they got a clear look, Bligh could see that her hands were bound in front of her, so that she could control the horse. She rode between the two men, with El Mexicano in front and Gilbourne behind. The outlaw was plainly guiding the group.

Night was coming on when the weather broke, and Arizona suddenly delivered one of its thunderous cascades of rain. Lightning flashed in the darkening skies and thunder volleyed like artillery. Against the still light western sky they could see a great pillar of dark rain advancing towards them, and had just time to ride up out of the gully and take cover under an overhanging slab of rock before it broke.

The twilight turned into a roaring world of water. The horses tucked themselves to the back of the overhang and though the men held on to their trailing reins, it was plain there was no real need. The animals had no intention of voluntarily going out into the storm.

Bligh unwrapped some strips of jerky and they chewed on the meat while the storm devoted itself to becoming more and more intense. The two gullies which ran down either side of their refuge first ran, then cascaded and finally roared with runoff water.

'Strange, is it not, that in this land which is waterless and parched, where a man can die very easily and very quickly of thirst, he could also die from drowning at a half hour's notice?' said Chavez, peering out from under their rock shelter. He opened his water bottle, drank what little remained, and held it under one of the dozen rivulets which cascaded from the rock above and past the open end of the shelter. It filled within minutes, and Bligh did the same.

By the time the storm was over, it was full dark. They had lost sight of the men and their victim and now they had also lost any chance of tracking them, for the cataracts of water would have washed out any tracks they might have left in the gullies between the rocks.

To try and catch up with the fugitives would be worse than useless; there were canyons and open cracks in the earth, by now made more dangerous by the water.

Bligh swore luridly and fumed inwardly but also in vain. The rain slackened into a downpour, and then to a steady beat. Chavez rolled himself in his blankets, propped his head on his bent forearm and was instantly asleep. Bligh stared at the hunched shape in the dark of the overhang, and settled down to be the guard.

The rain pattered on. When he could no longer keep his eyes open, Bligh elbowed Chavez into wakefulness and wrapped himself up his own blankets and slept.

The dawn came in to reveal a steaming landscape through which rivulets still ran, and the rocks glistened with water. The rain had stopped, but the sun had not yet had time to dry out the land, and the resulting humidity made them sweat even when they were sitting still under the rock.

Chavez lit a tiny fire and made coffee. They drank it, staring out at the landscape, which became clearer as the sun burned off the mist. It happened remarkably fast, as the heat sucked the dampness first out of the atmosphere and then out of the ground.

The rains had washed all the little pathways between the great boulders clean and left them floored with new sand. In the corners where the rocks joined, debris washed down the slopes had caught and made piles of rubbish. Tumbleweed piled its balls of needle sharp thorns in the gaps, and other debris caught on the thorns and roofed in the piles.

They stayed well clear of these debris. Among them, there could often be rattlesnakes which had been washed down with the thorns, and a rattler which had been half drowned and then thrown into a pile of thorns was a rattler in a furious temper.

They were just skirting one thorn-packed corner when Bligh's attention was caught by a corner of cloth sticking out from the pile. Gingerly, he extended his leg and caught the corner with a spur, and jerked at it. The cloth, part of a much larger piece of debris, was reluctant to be pulled, and he had to reach out and catch hold of it.

Instantly there was the dust-dry rustle of a rattlesnake's warning. Bligh jerked his hand back at once. Peering into the debris, he could not see the snake, though he could hear it, and it sounded close.

He dismounted and walked back down the narrow trail between the rocks until he came across a longer piece of broken ocotillo limb. The slender, thorn-studded pole was ideal for his purpose, and he took it back to the piece of cloth, twisted the pole in the cloth and drew it carefully out of the pile. The rattlesnake never stopped its warning, but still he could not tell where it was, but he realized he was probably looking directly at the reptile, but unable to see it because of the light and shadow dappling the hiding place.

At any rate, it did not strike, and he got the cloth out from the pile of tumbleweed and into the open. It was half of a man's fancy vest, sadly torn and stained from the flood, but recognizable none the less.

'It is the vest worn by Gilbourne, I think,' said Chavez, soberly. 'And it will have been carried straight down the line of little gullies to here. So we can trace it back to where Gilbourne lost it.'

They climbed the trail, looking around warily and found, as they climbed, various fragments of clothing, rent and ruined by the flood. There were sleeves and the collar from a black broadcloth coat, the other half of the vest, a boot made from what had once been fine leather.

What they were finding was, of course, Gilbourne's clothing. Bligh dreaded finding the girl's clothes, and was surprised at how much he cared about her fate. The higher they climbed the more he realized he was worried about her survival.

They found Gilbourne himself halfway to the top of the ridge, jammed between a rock and the side of the narrow gully. The flood had dealt cruelly with him and the stones and sand carried in the waters had torn and abraded his body sadly.

Chavez dismounted and approached it carefully, and leaned over to examine it more closely.

'Drowned, I guess,' Bligh said, dismounting, but the Mexican shook his head.

'No, *amigo*, he was shot,' he said. He prodded at the body with his knife and turned the ruined head over.

'See?' He pointed with the tip of the blade, and Bligh leaned over to look at a clean bullet hole in the temple. The slug, he realized on closer examination, had actually taken off the side of the man's head with its exit, but the face was intact enough to be recognized.

'When, do you think?' said Chavez. Bligh shook his head.

'Had to be last night. After the storm had finished, we'd have heard it, even down among those rocks. He was shot while the thunder was banging around, one more bang among so many,' he opined. Chavez nodded.

The man had been washed down from above, and to find from where, they followed the main line of the flood, tracing it from the sand and debris more or less straight up the narrow canyon. They found a couple of personal effects which must have been washed out of the pockets, including a draw-string bag containing gold coins and a few small gold nuggets, plus a thick gold ring with a black stone set in it.

'Seal ring,' said Bligh, examining the complicated crest carved deep in the stone. 'Wasn't his, that's for sure. I don't see friend Gilbourne as a renegade son of some noble house. Maybe the gold wasn't his, neither.'

They packed the stuff away into a saddle-bag and continued up the draw carefully, because neither of them wanted to be ambushed. Bligh said that so far as he was concerned, being killed from ambush was dying from stupidity.

Chavez agreed cautiously, without taking his eyes from the sides of the gully as they climbed. His attention was rewarded when he spotted a ribbon of black satin hanging from a rock halfway up the side of the cleft.

Bligh climbed up and recovered it. At first he thought it had been a woman's hair ribbon, but he could not remember Frankie wearing one. Then he realized he was looking at Gilbourne's tie.

'His necktie,' agreed Chavez. 'But how did it get so high? The water never got that far up. Look, you can see the mark.'

So, if Gilbourne had fallen down after he was shot – and if a practised bandit like El Mexicano had not relieved his victim of his money pouch – the body must have fallen out of his reach immediately it had been hit.

'He came from up there,' said Chavez. 'We must look higher.'

Together, they climbed the gully until it topped out halfway up the side of the mountain, and found no sign of a cave or overhang where the fugitives night have taken refuge and fallen out enough to kill.

'Let us try down the edge of the arroyo, here,' suggested the Mexican, and together they retraced the line of the cleft but up higher. They found nothing.

When they were above the point where the necktie had been caught on the canyon wall, they reined in and studied the lie of the land. They were on a thin rib of rock between two deep miniature canyons. The canyons followed roughly the same course, dropping steeply down the mountainside and into the tangle of massive boulders below.

They were only two of a system of small canyons which ran down the mountainside, and from above, it was clear that at this point, all the canyons took a sharp kink to follow the lie of the land. They were directly above one of these kinks, and the same thought struck both of them at the same time.

'He didn't fall on this side,' said Bligh. 'He was shot over that side, and the water carried him across the flood and hit this side. Then he was caught up by the rock, and the flood water stripped him. We're looking on the wrong side of the canyon!'

By the time they had retraced their steps the sun had climbed until it was at its highest in the sky. Both the men and the horses were in desperate need of a rest, and despite Bligh's uneasiness about the delay, they stopped again and watered their mounts from a huge puddle worn in the side of the mountain by years of floods.

The water was in the shade of a heavy overhang, and blessedly cool. Bligh checked for snakes, stripped to the waist and washed himself down. Chavez watched him do it and, when he had finished, handed Bligh the rifle and did the same thing himself. Finally, he plunged his head into the pool and shook his mane of hair like a great dog when he stood up.

'*Hombre!*' he said, gasping. 'That was good!'

His voice echoed strangely as he said it and both men noticed it. Bligh looked carefully at the overhang directly above the pool, where the shadows were deepest, then handed the rifle to Chavez, kicked off his boots and waded through the pool and climbed out the other side.

He was standing on a rock platform above the water, and at the back of it, the deep shadow concealed a gaping hole.

He waved to Chavez and stamped his feet back into his boots before drawing his gun and climbing the slope into the hole.

As soon as he got there, he could smell the pungent scent of old fires. Very cautiously, he started along the side of the rock. Out of the sun, it was very dark and he had to wait a little for his eyes to adjust. While he stood, listening intently, the smell of horses came to him.

Outside, there was a low whistle, and he covered one eye against the sunlight and ducked back to where he could be seen from across the pool. Chavez was standing with his rifle poised. Bligh waved, then ducked back into the cave mouth again.

He listened intently, but aside from the steady drip of water somewhere back in the hill, there was no sound. Finally, he struck a match on his thumbnail and held it up, away from his eyes.

The darkness in front of him was complete. Nowhere did the light reflect back to him. The silence continued.

Tentatively, he put forward one foot, and then the other. In the tiny light from his match he could see that he stood on a rocky floor. It was dry, so no water had flowed down it despite the storm the previous night. The smell of horses grew stronger. And with it the scent of old charcoal.

The match burned his fingers and he pinched it out. As he did so, he heard at the very edge of his hearing a sound like a sigh.

Instantly he threw himself down and rolled sideways, but there was no further sound, and no shot rang out. Feeling rather sheepish, he sat up and struck another match.

In front of him on the floor of the cave, lay a bundle. It was the size of a body wrapped in a blanket, and trussed with rope. It was very still.

CHAPTER ELEVEN

The match flickered out again, and Bligh lit another. This time he knew what he was looking for, and wasted none of his light searching. He reached out and probed the bound form on the floor and to his amazement, it twitched and a low moan came from the blankets.

There were the remains of a fire on the other side of it, and he got one of the half burned sticks to catch flame, and reached for the knots on the rope. Immediately, the bound form kicked wildly and emitted a series of choked, high-pitched screams.

'Frankie?' he asked, surprised. 'Frankie Lewis?'

The struggling stopped, and a low moan sounded. He reached for the knots on the part of the package he identified as the head, and stopped when she emitted several staccato sounds which sounded identifiably like: 'No! No!'

Nonplussed, he drew back and examined the parcel again, holding the stick closer to it for better light. In the glow, he could see squirming movement about halfway down the bound figure, where the hands should be. It was as though she was waggling a bullwhip haft under the blanket.

Or a snake.

With infinite care, he felt the moving folds, and found the writhing form of the snake. It was thick, as thick as his wrist, which meant that if this was a rattlesnake, it was a very big one indeed. What he could not understand was that if this was a rattler, why it was not sounding its rattle. Even muffled by the blanket, the sound would have carried recognizably.

A big snake would have a big bite, so he felt very gently along the snake from what seemed to be the tail end, moving about by the girl's calves up to the neck. The head seemed to be immobilized, and have a thick collar just below it, which twitched as he felt it. The muffled protest from beneath the blankets swelled.

She had to come out of there, and quickly. If she had been bitten by the rattler, he was surprised that she was still able to protest. But the longer he left it the more dangerous the poison would be. He felt around where her head should be, took out his bowie and slit the rope wrapped around it and peeled back the blanket gently.

When it came into the flickering light, he hardly recognized her. There was a tight gag around her mouth, so tight it had cut into her cheeks, and must have restricted her breathing.

She had her eyes tight shut, as she came into the dim light, and he reached under her head and undid the knot of the gag. It was caught in her hair, and he had to twist it free, which prompted an agonized gasp.

Even with the gag out, she was incapable of speech for a while, working her jaws and mouth. But when he reached down to cut the bonds round her arms, she managed to croak a strangled 'No!'

He went back to the cave mouth, to find there was no

sign of Chavez or their horses in the ravine. He shelved the worry at the back of his mind and dipped his bandanna in water from the pool and returned to the cave.

The relief on her face when he reappeared was dramatic. He squeezed the water into her mouth and swabbed round her face and neck while she was frantically trying to tell him something.

Finally, she got her throat to work, though rustily.

'Snake!' she croaked. 'Holding a snake! Help me, it's strong! But be careful, it's a rattler!'

He nodded and felt down the blankets until he could isolate the reptile's head. She was right, the snake was strong, and it was struggling madly to escape. Constricted by the blankets and the rope binding around them, it could only writhe and twist, but as soon as he cut those bindings, it would certainly be beyond the girl's strength to control it.

'I'll go for the head,' he told her, and saw panic flare in her eyes.

'If I cut it free lower down, it'll be able to fight you properly. Right now, he's got no leverage and he's tied down anyway. Once he's free to move, he'll bite the nearest thing – you! So keep hold while I get to his neck.'

He watched her fight back the panic, and nod abruptly, and felt her muscles tense as she took an even tighter hold on the snake. The reptile's struggles became even more frenzied and he knew she would lose hold any moment.

He felt back along the twisting body until he could feel the part just below her wrists. The snake was as immobile there as she could manage and, as he slipped the point of the bowie into the blankets, it too felt the approaching menace and gave a great shudder.

116

Even in the dim light, he saw her eyes widen and panic start, and, desperate, he thrust the point of the bowie under the writhing reptile, grabbed the head in his own left hand through the blankets, and ripped outwards in one long, slashing stroke.

The head came away in his hand, and the body went on rippling under the blankets for several seconds after it had been separated from the head. The girl closed her eyes and fell backwards inside the blankets, and for a dreadful moment he thought he had miscalculated and she was dead, struck in the reptile's dying spasms. – or, worse, that his desperate slash had severed her hand along with the snake's head.

Then she opened her eyes and let out one long, explosive sigh of relief.

'You,' she said, in a voice hoarse with emotion, 'took your goddamned time, Bligh!'

'Gee, thanks, ma'am,' he said, sarcastically. 'I like the way you cut away the "thanks for saving my life from a poisonous reptile" bit and get straight to the abuse. Saves all that time people waste in gratitude, when they get their lives saved.'

The next moment, he had his arms full of sobbing, quivering woman, and was holding her body tight against his.

He let her sob until the first storm of shock had passed, and she relaxed in his arms. She smelled of horses and sweat and having spent too long in the same clothes without a chance to change. He was faintly surprised to find a woman can smell like a man after a hard day's work.

She didn't feel like one, though, and he had had to disengage himself from her while he rekindled the remains of the fire and added to it from a pile of wood stacked against the cave wall. When it was burning brightly enough to work by, he cut the bonds and she was able to draw up her knees and kick away blankets and ropes, and mixed in among them, the body of the snake.

He pulled it out and examined it, careful to shake the head out of the blanket and keep his hands away from the open mouth.

It was a big diamond-back rattlesnake and its rattle had been muffled with a length of hide knotted tightly around it. Thick, strong and powerful, it had been a miracle that the girl had been able to hold it still even with both hands, and the body largely immobilized by the bonds and blankets.

'A big one,' he said soberly. 'How long had you been holding that?'

She shuddered, and the shudder turned into a spell of uncontrollable shaking. He held her again until she had quietened, then she sat upright and began to pull out her hair from its bird's nest tangle into a braid.

He asked again how long she had been bound up with the snake. She thought for a moment, then shook her head.

'What time is it now?' she said. He told her, and she nodded.

'We took shelter here last night when the rain started,' she said. 'El Mexicano – you know he's an American, of course, you saw him in Tucson, didn't you? Well, he was aiming for somewhere further back in the hills, but the storm took him by surprise.

'So we came in here. It seems to have been used by many people, not just him. There's another entrance

118

further back there, big enough to bring horses in.'

As she spoke, a stone rattled somewhere in the dark, and Chavez's voice called, '*Hola*, the fire!'

'Come on in,' Bligh called and the Mexican came from the darkness. He was leading their horses in single file, and dropped the reins to ground-hitch them.

'I was worried I had lost you, *amigo*,' he said. 'With the *bandido* somewhere around I did not want to leave the horses and, when I looked around, I found this entrance. From above, it is clear to see.'

Bligh told him about finding the girl and her deadly blanket mate and the Mexican shook his head in amazement.

'He is a devil, that one,' he said. 'But why bind you up with a snake? He could have killed you easily himself.'

She looked startled. 'Oh, the snake was not for me,' she said. 'He thought it would bite me right away, yes. But the reason he left a live rattler was for you two – particularly for Tom Bligh, here. He hates him.'

Chavez was appalled at the cruelty of binding the girl up with a live rattlesnake, just to turn her into a living booby-trap, and he treated her with old-world courtesy. Bligh was slightly nettled to see she responded to it warmly. The feeling surprised him, for he was not used to being jealous over a woman. In his life women were either ranchers' wives like Winnie Bedford, or dance hall girls. Only a husband could be jealous over Winnie, and there was not the slightest point in being possessive over dance-hall girls.

Frankie, though, was a new experience to him. He had seen women gamblers before, though they were uncommon, but never come across one he liked as much. Their calling usually made women who worked in saloons hard and calculating. They had a professional practised charm if they were clever, and none at all if they were not.

Frankie, though, was different. While Chavez filled their coffee pot and made coffee, Bligh unwrapped his skillet and sliced bacon into it. While he was doing it, he was surprised to find Frankie getting the ingredients together and making camp-fire bread from his stores. She did it without fuss, and with a quiet expertise which made him wonder, and when it was finished and cooked on the hot stones, it was very good.

And this was the young woman who had been tied up with an angry rattlesnake for company, strong enough to keep it from biting her and strong-willed enough to handle it when she had to.

'She is quite a woman, this one,' Chavez murmured in his ear, when Frankie went off to wash and tidy herself up. 'I think you could be a very lucky man, *amigo*. But I would not play her at cards, if I were you.'

Bligh glanced at him, surprised. 'You think she cheats?'

'I think she does not need to cheat, my friend. I think she is clever enough not to need to. Remember what I say. It will be good for you in the future.'

He chuckled and wiped his plate with the last of his bread, then went off to wash it in the water hole. When Bligh brought the rest of the cooking gear, he was scrubbing out the plate with sand from the bottom of the pool and shooting the dirty water over the edge of the ledge.

When they got back to the fire, Frankie was finished and Bligh was surprised at how much difference a few minutes' fussing had wrought. She looked clean, her hair was pulled into a thick pigtail and she had made herself a cloak and hood with one of the blankets. He dug into his saddle bags and handed her his spare shirt.

'Ain't fancy, but it'll keep the sun from your shoulders,' he told her. And she turned away to put it on over the low-necked dress.

'One thing,' said Chavez as she buttoned it up. 'Why did they fall out, El Mexicano and Gilbourne? I thought they were partners.'

'So did Gilbourne,' said the girl with a tight, savage grin. 'It was a bigger surprise to him than to anybody else. The outlaw just followed him out to the pool when he went to get water, and I heard a shot. He came back alone and reloaded his gun. When I asked, he just shrugged and said he saw no reason to split the money.

'He does not think twice about killing; it is like taking a deep breath, to him.'

'What we need to know now,' Bligh said, 'is where the renegade went.'

'Oh, I reckon I can tell you that,' she said. 'At any rate, where I think he will go. He'll be heading for that big rock pillar on the trail up to Dragoon Station.'

Chavez and Bligh stared at her. 'The one called Spanish Spike? How do you know?'

'Because that's where I told him I hid the money. I made a deal with him. I told him where the money was and he would not put my feet in the fire, or shoot me.'

'Just tie you up with a rattler!'

She shrugged. 'I hadn't thought of that. Nor anything else. I thought I had bought my life, not just invented a new way of dying. Kind of stupid, really. If he would kill his partner rather than split, why let the witness live? – particularly one who knew where the money was.'

'So what did you tell him?'

'I thought he would take me with him to show him where the money was. Instead, he laughed and said he knew just where it would be. He thought it was very funny, then he caught the rattler outside, and when he wrapped me up with it, he was laughing so much, he could hardly talk.'

Chavez muttered, '*Madre de Dios!*' and she shot a look at him.

'I do not think he has much to do with God, *señor*,' she said. 'More like the Devil. I know. Believe me, I know!'

She mounted up behind Bligh when they left the cave, and he found he liked the feeling of arms wound round his waist.

CHAPTER TWELVE

Coming down from among the rocks and making for Spanish Spike was a deal quicker than tracking El Mexicano and his prisoners when they were going the other way. The outlaw was not slowed by the need to keep the girl under his eye now, and he did not have to worry about getting a bullet in the back from his enforced partner, either.

He had made good time, but so did they. Threading their way among the rocks down from the place Cochise had made his stronghold, they turned into the road and followed the wheel ruts towards Dragoon Station.

Even before they could see the rock post sticking out of the desert, they were aware they were not alone. First Chavez whistled shrilly and jerked his head towards the hillside on their south side. From one of the canyons leading down through the rocks, dust was rising, and Bligh closed up on the Mexican and rode alongside.

From behind his left ear, Frankie's voice said, matter of factly, 'Yes, I can see it, too. Lot of dust for one man. Does he have a gang somewhere?'

Bligh did not think so. The man was plainly a loner, and trying to ally with him looked like a fatal error, to judge

123

from Gilbourne's end. It was far more likely that the dust was being raised by Apaches coming down from the hills, there. In theory, they were all making their way to the reservation on the San Carlos, but there were bound to be dissidents, young hotheads and old plotters.

They rode on along the road, aware of their own dust, and watching the approaching dust from the hills. Because he was a local and had experience with the Apaches Bligh also kept a wary eye to the other points of the compass. Whoever was coming down from the hills was making little effort to conceal their progress which was not like Apaches.

That would have been difficult at the best of times, though the night's rain had laid the dust to a large extent, but the Indians could keep the signs of their passing down when they chose. It made for slow progress, and the approaching horsemen whoever they were, showed no sign of even trying to conceal their presence.

Even taking his greatest care, he must have missed something, because suddenly, the high ridge to their south was crowned with men on horses. They made no attempt to come down on to the road, but simply kept pace with Bligh and his companions. They were Apaches, sure enough. Apache men, with no women or children in their group.

Indians did that when they expected a chase. Its purpose was to make the quarry run and run hard, to take the edge off the horses' endurance. The pursuers did not even have to try and keep up with the quarry. All it took was a few warriors riding easily alongside, while the rest followed on, their horses hardly stretching themselves.

Sooner or later, the quarry's mounts tired, and the

Indians caught up. The trick was not to run until some end – a river crossing, a natural strong point, or some escape route – was in reach, and then go like the very devil.

Luckily, Chavez was of the same mind, and the two cantered easily along the road, uncaring of the dust which began to come up as the surface dried out, but keeping the Apaches to their right.

'Don't let them get me,' Frankie panted in his ear. He could hear the tension in her voice, and feel it in her tightened grip, so he understood it. But he was still surprised at the Indians' behaviour. Any Apaches left in these hills now that he had seen the families moving north were either dissidents on a hold-out against the troops, or stragglers.

The party which was keeping pace with them seemed to be neither. They had already ignored two chances to pour down the slope and engulf Bligh and his party, so they did not seem to be hunting swift scalps. Yet there were no women or children with them, and so far as he could see, each of the warriors was carrying a rifle. An Apache would give his eye teeth for a Winchester or a Henry repeater. The repeating carbines were being issued to the US Cavalry in the region to replace their single shot weapons, and the idea of having eleven or even fifteen shots in their hands instead of one appealed to every Indian.

Any amnesty would include a surrender of weapons, he knew.

Chavez said, 'I thought the Apaches were being taken to their reservation? They say in Tucson the troubles are over. The Indian wars are finished.'

Bligh grunted agreement. 'Geronimo was the last of them, and he went down into Mexico, last I heard. That ain't Geronimo's bunch, anyways. We'd never have seen them, we'd just be dead.'

The girl quivered when he said it, and he cursed himself for his stupidity. She was frightened enough without his pessimism. He stared hard up the slope towards the slow-moving Indians, then gave a surprised snort.

The girl's arms tightened. 'Are they coming?' she said, in a tight, strained voice. He shook his head.

'No, they ain't. They're going!' he told her. 'Look up now.'

She twisted to look up the slope and gaped as the line of warriors one by one dropped out of sight at the far side of the ridge. The last one pulled his horse to a standstill and looked directly down at them. Then he raised his rifle over his head and shook it, giving a series of high, yipping yells at the same time. Finally, he wheeled his mount and disappeared in pursuit of his comrades.

Chavez let out a hissing explosion of breath, and dropped his Winchester back into its saddle-boot. Bligh shook his head and chuckled. Frankie gave a convulsive jerk.

'What in the name of all that's holy was all that about – and why are you laughing?' she hissed in Bligh's ear. 'We just nearly got attacked by Apaches.'

Bligh twisted in the saddle to see into her furious face.

'You, girl, just seen one of the rarest things in this Territory,' he told her. 'You've just seen an Apache joke. And those are as rare as hens' teeth!'

She stared at him, then quite unexpectedly drew back her fist and punched him, hard, in the shoulder.

'Joke? You call that a joke?' she said. 'They just frightened the bejeezus out of me, and you think that's funny?'

126

'Not me,' he said, rubbing his bruised shoulder. 'But they did. Right now, the loudest noise them Apaches are making is a belly laugh. Tell me, can you see any dust now? Which way did they go? Can you tell me?'

She stared up at the ridge. Above it the air was clear and clean without a sign of dust.

'There's nothing!' she said, amazed. 'Where did they go? They were raising enough dust for a regiment when they came down the mountains – and now, nothing! Where are they?'

He shrugged. 'They ain't down here, lighting slow fires, that's all I care about. Reason there ain't no dust sign is they don't want there to be any. Either that or they ain't moving. Just waiting for us to go away. I thought there was too much dust in the air when they come down the mountains for the number of horses.'

'So?'

'So they wanted us to see them coming, and run scared. That would have made an Apache warrior laugh. When we didn't run, the joke was over, and they went away. Likely on their way to the San Carlos after all, but took time out to give us a scare.'

Chavez shot him a hard look. 'If they wanted to give us a scare, *amigo*, they did a good job on me. I was scared all right. Now, let us put some distance between them and us in case they want another laugh. Where is this Spanish Spike we seek. I don't need more jokes.'

Bligh pointed. 'There,' he said, and they turned and looked up the trail to where the thick column of rock showed over the shoulder of the next rise.

The rock was a tall, thick finger standing alone among a tumble of massive boulders. What had made it develop

127

so very differently from the other boulders in the area, Bligh did not know. But it was unique, an unmissable landmark in a landscape packed with remarkable features.

Frankie chuckled.

'We stopped there because Gilbourne asked them to,' she said. 'That's what made it easier to convince that bandit. He knew we had stopped there. When I told him I hid the money there, he just nodded and started to tie me up again. Then he got the snake.'

Bligh could feel the quiver in her body when she mentioned the rattler, but she pulled herself away and cleared her throat.

'Now, I want to see you kill another rattler – that snake!' she said. 'Let's go – he's had a long enough start.'

But when they pulled up at the foot of Spanish Spike, there was no sign of the outlaw. Bligh, who had led them on a circuitous route to avoid being seen while they were still too far away to be of any use, pulled up and let the girl down.

'Where did you send him?' he asked, wiping his hat band with his bandanna. The material was showing signs of the heat of the day.

'I just told him it was at Spanish Spike,' she said, looking puzzled. 'He didn't even ask me for details, just laughed and tied me up with that darned snake. After that I wasn't in any state to tell him anything. I was gagged and holding the rattler and wondering where the hangment you were.'

Chavez remounted his horse and set off round the foot of the rock, hanging sideways to try and pick up tracks. Bligh watched him go, then started doing the same thing in the opposite direction, but on foot and leading the

128

mount. Frankie trailed behind him, keeping out of the way of his tracking.

They had gone about halfway round the rock when Chavez appeared from the other side. He, too, was leading his horse now, and examining the ground at every step.

'*Nada!*' he said disgustedly. 'Not a sign. Nothing has come by this rock since before the rain last night. I stake my life on it. No horse, no man. Not even an Indian.'

They stood together, then Bligh climbed back on to his horse and started doing a second circuit, going in the opposite direction and staying further out from the base of the rock.

It was a long, hot process. By now it was late afternoon, and the sun was lower in the sky, throwing the ruts and dimples in the ground into high relief. Ripples in the sandy soil invisible when the sun was at its height suddenly came out at him now that the sun turned them into patterns of light and shadow.

He found the tracks when he was halfway round, and he found them in the few minutes of the setting of the sun when the light lay almost horizontally along the ground.

El Mexicano had done a fine job of hiding his tracks, and Bligh was torn between admiration for the man and sullen fury that he had been so completely misled.

The bandit had used an old enough trick, the simple expedient of dragging a rolled blanket behind himself to fill in the hoofprints in the sandy soil. But he had also pulled the blanket from side to side as he went, to avoid making a flat and direct path.

As he followed the track to the foot of the mesa, Bligh saw it snuff out as the sun dipped below the horizon, and left them in the sudden dark silence of an Arizona sunset.

The afterglow was fading when Chavez and the girl joined him, and he led them away from the rock to a pile of broken stones a little further along the trail. They ground hitched the horses, and hunkered down in a little natural hollow in the stone. Last night's rain had wetted the sand here, and there was still a little cool damp coming up through the ground, held there by the shadow during the day.

'So, where is he now?' Chavez asked, running his tongue along the edge of a cigarette paper, and twirling the end to keep the tobacco from running out. Bligh hunkered down.

'We'll find out in the morning,' he said. 'Wasn't light enough to see whether he left tracks away from the rock as well as going in. We don't even know if the tracks we found was coming or going, anyways. Could have been either.'

'Or both,' said Frankie. She had pulled her skirt up to her knees and ripped off a strip of her underskirt, with which she was engaged in cleaning her little revolver. How it had survived the process of being captured along with her, tied up in the blanket with her and the snake, and then riding behind Bligh for a full day, was a mystery, but survive it had, and she handled it like an experienced shot.

Bligh nodded soberly. 'True,' he said. 'Or even neither. He didn't sign his tracks. Could have been somebody else. One of the Indians we saw earlier on, for instance. Or a passer-by. Could even have been you.'

Her head jerked up at that, and her eyes flashed in the moonlight. 'Me?'

'Sure,' he said, affably. 'You, ma'am. When you hid the money you got out of the strongbox. I don't know how you

130

got it, and I don't know where you got it, but get it you did. Didn't you?'

The silence was confirmation enough. The moon was up now, and he could see her face in stark tones of black and silver. It was like a theatrical mask he had seen on the proscenium arch at a real theatre in Santa Fe. Beautiful but unmoving and strangely inhuman.

'How did you know?' she asked suddenly, and Chavez gave a grunt of confirmation.

'*Amigo*,' he said. 'You are serious about this?'

Bligh nodded. It had to be her. El Mexicano had not had time to get to the stage office to recover his cash when he fled from Tucson because of the sudden flare of recognition in Bligh's face. He must have put the money into the company's box before Bligh saw him the previous night. Since then he had been on the run, first to Dragoon station to recover his money, then to Tombstone to make contact with his partner when he had failed to find the cash.

'So far as he was concerned, the money was in the strongbox. No wonder he didn't push things when I shot at him back near Maricopa. His cash was as safe with Wells Fargo as it would have been anywhere else. Safer – because the company always has a guard on the stage.'

In the silence which followed, the click as she closed the action on her newly loaded gun was unnaturally loud. He watched her carefully, but all she did was push the weapon into her waistband and wipe her hands on the remains of her strip if petticoat.

'But he shot the guard on the first stage hold-up,' she said reasonably. 'Otherwise the hold-up would have been successful. He could have got his money back.'

Bligh bent forward and piled up a few sticks he took from his blanket roll. Shielding the match with his hands, he struck a flame and coaxed the little pile of wood and kindling into life, deep among the rocks where it could be seen only from close by. Chavez made a startled movement when he struck the match, but relaxed again as he put it into the kindling. It caught on the bone dry material and a tiny flame started in the midst of the fire.

'Best sit back from the fire against the rocks,' he said, pinching out the match immediately. 'He may be able to see it from where he is. Don't give him a silhouetted target. He's a good shot. Let's hope he is also a very strung-up one.'

The shot came from an unexpected quarter. He had expected El Mexicano to be on or near the pillar of rock, but instead the shot came from outside their perimeter, in the broken rocky ground to the east.

It hit near the fire and howled off into the night with a banshee screech. The ricochet was followed by several more measured shots, and only a sharp warning from Chavez stopped Bligh trying to return the fire.

'He cannot see us, so he wishes to observe our muzzle flashes and locate us,' she Mexican said. It made perfect sense, for the shots from outside were obviously searching fire. No two bullets struck in the same place.

Bligh was staring out at the night time blackness, trying to pick out a muzzle flash without success when the girl nudged him and pointed. He followed the shadowy line of her arm and saw, against the bulk of a rocky outcrop, the tell-tale flash.

It illuminated little, but the flash itself was a curious shape. He kept his eyes glued to the spot over the next two shots, and realized the man was firing from behind two rocks, through the sharp V between them. The chances of hitting him with a return shot were remote at best, and would be revealing of their own position if nothing else.

This man was too good a shot to take the risk, and regretfully, he decided not to shoot back until he was certain of the target.

The searching shots went on for another ten minutes or so, spaced and measured, then stopped.

By now the moon was completely up, sailing huge and bright over the landscape. It turned the rocks an eerie shade of silver, and the shadows to charcoal. All three of them watched towards the source of the searching fire until their eyes watered, but the silver landscape was still and unbroken. If El Mexicano were out there, stalking them, he was doing it in total silence, and without betraying movement.

Taking it in turns, one at a time with the other two watching, they slept fitfully. It was not restful but it was better than nothing.

CHAPTER THIRTEEN

Bligh wakened the other two in the faint light of the false dawn. The sun would be up shortly but at this moment the fading dark of night cloaked the land and made it mysterious.

Quietly, they saddled the horses, gave them water from the canteens and led them quietly out of their circle of rocks and rode along the foot of the tower which was the Spanish Spike. The cold of night still left a chill on the air, but the faint glow in the sky to the east told them the dawn itself was not far away.

They managed to round the base of the rock without damage and Bligh dropped from his mount to the ground. Chavez took up the lead and led the girl away round the detritus slope, while Bligh dropped back, crept through the boulders and, hugging the wall of the pinnacle, made his way back to where he had seen the muzzle flashes in the dark. He had no idea whether the bandit was still in his place, but he needed to know if the man was not there, because that meant he was out somewhere in the open.

The back of his neck itched almost unbearably, an old sign of danger but one which was also infuriatingly unreliable. It told him nothing except that he was risking his life, and generally he knew that already.

It took him twenty minutes or so to get to the vantage point he had chosen, behind and above the notch between the two boulders through which he had seen El Mexicano's muzzle flashes last night. From here, he could see down to their campsite, and on the boulders which formed its natural rampart, the two rocks he had left there as direction markers.

When they lined up, he knew he was looking down the bandit's line of aim.

The man must have been shooting from a point directly below and in front of him. To choose his shooting stand, the bandit must have picked it out before dark, and left himself some aiming markers, and after a little casting around with infinite caution, he reckoned he must be directly above and behind the man's vantage point.

He lay against a boulder, and listened intently for sounds of movement, but heard none. When he was sure he was not going to get any more clues, he stepped with infinite care on to a smaller rock, and eased himself on to the top of the boulder.

El Mexicano must last night have been directly in front of him. He could see between the boulders and pick out his marker rocks clearly.

He braced his feet carefully, pulled the rifle to his shoulder, and stood up. The sights lined up perfectly on a little hollow directly below and in front of him, and he could see quite clearly in the clean dawn light the twinkle of brass cartridge cases strewn around the sniper's nest.

It was otherwise empty.

Without pausing, he threw himself off the top of the

rock and into the little depression. As he dropped, he quite clearly heard the faint, waspish buzz of a bullet past his ear, close enough to feel its passing puff of air. The report followed immediately, and somewhere above and behind him – frighteningly close behind him – he heard the slug crack viciously into the rock he had just left.

His own rifle was unfired, and the shot must have come from directly in front of him, since it had passed through the same V-shaped cleft between the rocks that the sniper had used last night. Therefore, the shooter must be in – or directly in line with – the same position Bligh and his companions had occupied last night, and he repaid the shot with another, along the same line.

He saw quite clearly one of his marker rocks explode into a puff of dust and disappear, and repeated the shot to destroy the other. It was a simple act of frustration, and the shot in any case missed, but it shifted El Mexicano, for there was no follow-up shot and, after a moment, he heard a horse's hoofs rattling on the stone, and some dust rose up along the base of the rock pillar.

Whatever else he was, El Mexicano was a professional. He was a good stalker, a remarkable shot – if Bligh had not thrown himself off the rock instantly when he found the hollow empty, he would by now be dead – and he knew when to abandon a plan which had not worked out, before it became a death-trap.

The trouble was that he, Bligh, did not know where the bandit had gone, but he did know that he had ridden off in the tracks of Chavez and Frankie. They must have been alerted by the shot, but they had no way of knowing who had fired it: Bligh or El Mexicano.

Bligh clambered out of the little depression and ran

136

down the hill as fast as he could. It was a risky business. The ground was a clutter of broken rocks as big as a man, tumbled and crowded, piled into untidy heaps and often balanced precariously on one another. Every time his foot hit the rock slide, he risked being pitched on to a jagged boulder, or, worse, starting a minor rockslide which would cripple or even engulf him.

Twice he took flight from a rock to feel it tip under his weight, and hear it crash behind him. Once, in its fall, a man-sized boulder flicked his heel and sent him sprawling on the top of the next slab.

In his crazy rush, he twice heard shots echo ahead of him and swore foully to himself. But he kept going. He had nowhere else to go.

The headlong rush took him off the tumbled scree and on to firmer ground. It was still uneven and stony, but this section was stable, and he made better time over it.

Even so, it was nearly an hour before he got back to the point where he had left Chavez and the girl, and he swore to himself when he saw one horse standing alone, ground hitched, nuzzling at a shapeless bundle lying on the ground.

He approached cautiously, searching the foot of the great rock pillar for signs of an ambush. He could see none, but El Mexicano was a skilful stalker, and he did not seriously expect to find anything obvious.

But no shot banged out when he stood up and walked to the horse. The shape lying at its feet was Chavez. There was blood by his head, and the battered sombrero had a hole in it. Bligh dropped to is knees next to the body, still searching the rocks with his eyes, and fumbled at the throat for a pulse.

It was there, all right, and to his amazement, it was strong and steady. Even as he felt the neck, Chavez moved slightly, and said in a muffled voice, 'Ah, *hombre*, I didn't know you cared!'

The wound in his head was messy, and had bled a lot like all head wounds, but it was slight. The bullet must have barely grazed him, though it had slashed across his scalp leaving a wound like a knife. The shock must have knocked him out, but it had not lasted. He was even comparatively clear-headed. They bound up the wound with his own bandanna and he managed to balance his sombrero on the bandage which held it in place.

His story was predictable. They had heard the shots exchanged between El Mexicano and Bligh, and waited by their horses for Bligh to return. Chavez had not wanted to leave the girl by herself while he went to investigate, reasoning that if Bligh had been successful, he would find them himself, and if the bandit had ambushed Bligh successfully, they did not want to walk into the same trap.

'And then the girl, she scream, and the lights, they go out,' Chavez finished. He drank from the remaining canteen and passed it to Bligh. The water was brackish and warm, but it was better than nothing. Just. Bligh would have given his right arm for a pot of strong coffee.

All their pursuit, their tracking and their work had been for nothing. They were back exactly where they had been two days ago. The girl was in the hands of El Mexicano, they were no closer to finding the money, and the bandit was away and clear.

Quite clearly the bandit had not recovered the money, or he would not have bothered to hang around. He therefore thought that Frankie was his only lead to it, which was why he had kidnapped her again. For a moment, Bligh wondered as he had done before whether she was in fact in league with El Mexicano, but the rattlesnake had been real enough and so had her terror.

It was pointless asking Chavez which way El Mexicano and his prisoner had gone, because he had been unconscious when they left. Bligh himself knew they had not gone back along the base of the mesa because that was the way he had come.

So they had either headed north or followed the line of the great rock round. There was not enough soft ground to take a hoofprint, and the stones were too tumbled to show the scrapes of a horseshoe, so it was a matter of guesswork.

'I reckon he followed on round the cliff to the east,' he told Chavez and the Mexican nodded, then winced as his head protested.

'I guess so, *amigo*,' he said. 'He thinks me dead, perhaps, and he does not know whether you are wounded or not. I think he goes to the east, too.'

So to the east they went. That way and to the south lay first Dragoon Station, and Tombstone and eventually the Chiricahua Mountains, with their savage beauty and savage people. Beyond that, came the border with New Mexico Territory, and the US Cavalry outpost at Fort Bowie hanging in the throat of Apache Pass.

El Mexicano might intend going that way into New Mexico and swinging south to Mexico itself. But he would not, could not, take the girl with him as a prisoner.

He did not like following blindly, but he had no choice. Doing his best to search for sign he let Chavez ride and

139

tracked on foot. His boots, high-heeled and narrow for riding, chafed his feet sadly, and the heat of the day was already building to its noon high.

He found his first true sign an hour later, a fresh scrape mark left by a horseshoe on a flat plate of rock. It had not been there two nights ago, because the rain would have washed the scratched dust out of it. Therefore it was left this morning, within the last couple of hours.

He signed to Chavez and followed the line of the mark. Within a few yards, he picked up another, and couple of hundred yards further on, several at once.

When they came abreast of a gap between two vast boulders, he hesitated. The vestige of the trail led on past the gap, but there was a scrap of bright, fine cotton caught on the rough edge of the broken boulder to one side. It was the same shade as the petticoat scraps Frankie had used to clean her little revolver.

But were they meant to follow it, or was it a warning? He raised his rifle and cocked it, held it pistol fashion in his right hand and slipped sideways between the rocks. Chavez dismounted and followed him.

The gap between the boulders was obviously used by more than one group as passageway. In the silt which had built up in the narrow floor there were the tracks of both men and horses. One of them was of Bligh's own mount, taken away along with the girl. At the other side, the pathway spread out and so did the tracks. He lost the way twice, fuming at himself for his slowness but forced to go cautiously by the terrain. Every rock provided a hiding place, every kink in the trail, and there were many, suggested a possible ambush.

He could see above the rocks that the mountainside

opened out just here, and supposed that straight downhill from their position was the stage route and ultimately Dragoon Springs.

He was about to step out towards it when he put his foot on a loose stone, his ankle turned and threw him forward against the rock.

As he did so, there was a fountain of dust from the rock next to his head and a ricocheting bullet squealed away into the canyon behind. He heard Chavez swearing as the horse, startled, bucked, throwing him against the stone in the narrow space.

Pumping the carbine's action to jack another shell into the breech, he saw a flicker of movement on top of one of the giant boulders on the downhill side. He flicked the weapon to his shoulder and fired in the same instant, pumping it again and yet a third time. Two of the shots whined off the rocks, the third made no sound, but the head he had noticed over the boulder disappeared.

From down the canyon, a horse's hoof-beats rattled and a girl screamed shrilly. The horse, running wildly, came round the corner and headed for its only way out – the gap in which Bligh was now stood.

There was not room for them both, and the horse was showing no sign of slowing. He could see the girl bouncing ungainly in the saddle, though she did not seem to have hold of the reins,

There was no way out. Chavez was blocking the trail behind him, the bolting horse in front.

But the horse was his. A trained cowpony, able to turn on a dollar, to stop in its tracks to snub down a running steer and hold it against braced legs.

He stuck two fingers in his mouth and blew like a steam

141

whistle. The horse simply stopped, dead. Frankie Lewis came sailing over its head, howling, like a leaping panther. And landed squarely on top of Bligh.

There had been times when Bligh had wondered what it would be like to have Frankie's generous curves all over him. She was a woman of her time, full fleshed and all curves.

But that flesh and those curves travelling at only a slightly lesser speed than the galloping horse, hit him like a howitzer shell.

He went down like a pine in an avalanche, full length on the ground. His Winchester was knocked out of his hands and rattled against the wall. His head, only slightly cushioned by his hat, struck the floor of the canyon with a smack which made it ring like a chow triangle. With several stones of wriggling woman flesh on top of him, he was effectively pinned to the ground, even if he had felt inclined to get up.

Frankie was as winded as he. She writhed like a hooked trout, gasping for breath but apparently unable to get off him. Bligh, impacted by her weight, was just as winded.

Above his head he could hear rattling hoofs and then a gun banged out, but he had no idea as to whose gun it might be. A horse – Chavez's mount, it turned out later, was prancing all round him like a dancehall girl – and Chavez himself was shouting incoherently.

Eventually, the noise ran down. The shooting stopped, Chavez's horse came to a standstill and shivered like a plague victim. Frankie got her breath back in one huge gasp and then spent it all in a stream or profanity which would have made a range segundo blush, and Bligh managed to get his hand on his gun.

He pushed Frankie off him and sat up, searching the canyon walls for sign of the bandit. They remained bare and innocent.

The runaway horse was standing where it had been told, head down and flanks heaving slightly, and Chavez's horse was still quivering.

Bligh realized that his left thigh was a mass of pain, and for a moment thought it was broken. But when he straightened his leg gingerly, there was no scrape of broken bone or noticeable shortening. He felt round the painful area carefully and found only a fast swelling bruise and muscles which worked only under angry protest.

He pulled Frankie upright, recovered his knife from his boot, and cut her hands free. They were tied behind her back, and had gone so dark they were almost black with engorged blood. The binding had been savagely tight, and intended to cause pain.

She was a poor sight. Her face was badly bruised and he could see the bruising getting worse by the second. She must have landed on it, unable to break her fall with anything but Bligh himself. And for that they had both paid.

Chavez had dismounted to help, but he was mainly concerned with keeping an eye on the canyon rim where the bandit had disappeared. He reached up and unhooked their single canteen from the saddle horn and passed it down to them, and Frankie took a swig and then spat it over her swollen hands. It did not look as though it helped much. Bligh swallowed his ration, and retrieved his Winchester.

The weapon was scratched, but the Winchester was a robust weapon, and when he worked the action it obediently threw one cartridge out of the slot and fed in another. There was no discernible bend in the barrel and the sights were intact.

'*Señorita*,' said Chavez, 'do you know where he would go to now, this man?' She shot him a look which would have skinned a bear.

'Why, sure,' she said bitterly. 'In the time I was waiting to be rescued by my regular rescue team, we talked of little else! I gathered it is nice in Madrid at this time of year, and Paris, France, has its attractions. Myself, I was in favour of good old New York. Where would you recommend?'

Bligh thought she might have shown more gratitude, but he realized she had not had a good morning.

CHAPTER FOURTEEN

El Mexicano lay on the ledge halfway up the pillar of rock and sweated. Soon, now, the moving sun would round the pillar and fall directly upon him and his choice would be to stay where he was and fry or try to get down and make a run for it without his enemies noticing.

He was not a Mexican, though he did nothing to dispel the myth and the name which had grown up around it. He came from County Durham in England via the Royal Navy, having signed up to avoid a prison sentence for armed robbery. He had jumped ship in Jamaica during a fever scare, signed on an American trading schooner and found himself in the United States.

He was a tall man and a strong one, and his will was as strong as his shoulders. He had lived on his wits and other people's money for so long now, that he had forgotten the grindingly hard work that those other people had to put in to earn their money. Not that he was afraid of hard work. He was realistic enough to realize that he often worked harder to steal less money than he could have earned in the same time by honest means.

The truth was that the thought that he was profiting from other men's efforts gave him pleasure. He considered honesty a weakness and honest men his natural prey.

Mostly, he did not care what harm he did them and their families. There had been a time when he, too, had worked for his bread. Besides his term in the Royal Navy, he had been a cowhand, a teamster, and a trapper, but his brutal nature had driven him from one job after another. Jobs working with stock in the Territories were not easy to get because the smaller ranchers mainly did their own day-to-day work, and could afford hired help only when they needed it or could not do without it. The larger ranchers usually had their own tried and trusted long-term hands.

Also there was the matter of his reputation. He knew because he had been forced to realize it, that although white men and their settlements tended to be few and far between out here beyond the United States' western boundaries, those same few men tended to know one another, or of one another quite well.

There was little to do when riding night herd, or around a camp-fire of an evening, or over a bar at any time of day, but talk. Men talk of the things they know: of cattle and hunting, of mining and ranching, where to find good water and avoid bad. Of fighting against Indians, who naturally enough resisted with bitter fury the theft of their hunting ground, the abuse of their women and the slaughter of their children. Men's lives were a constant fight, against the country, the drought and the floods, and even against one anther.

They exchanged warnings and knowledge, too. The savage bear which ranged a particular corner of the mountains, the fact that the creeks were low up in the hills, and the rains were late this year.

And they warned one another against the equally savage men who thought the world was an open treasury for them to plunder at will. Without ever laying eyes on him, men from one end of the Territories to the other knew about El Mexicano.

So he kept from them the fact that he was not Mexican at all, but English. His bizarre mask-cum-hood and his carefully chosen small arms and the clothing he wore for his raids covered his real identity without covering his character one little bit.

He was known as a ruthless man, with a brutal nature and a total lack of conscience. He would rob a nun with as little compunction as he would rob a banker. It did not matter how much or how little each of his victims owned, he would take it all. Resistance was met with brutality at best, death at worst.

He was not used to losing, and he was infuriated by frustration, and at the moment he was suffering the effects of both.

He wanted, in short, to kill. The only thing which stayed his hand, apart from the fact that the rancher from the stage and the Mexican who rode with him were surprisingly hard to shake off or kill, was the fact that the damned woman card player knew where his loot was hidden and she refused to tell him.

He could have made her talk, he was sure. But she had been tougher than he had expected. The rattlesnake he had used both as a way of executing her and ambushing anybody who tried to rescue her had not, for some reason, worked. And the fear of it had not unbuttoned her stubborn mouth.

Now, she and the rancher were back together and, as a bonus, the damned Mexican was with her as well. He could kill them all at the same time.

Down on the detritus slope, stones rattled and he hunched his rifle into his shoulder, and eased back the hammer. They were coming, and they would come through the gap between the great boulders he had selected for his killing ground.

There was no way round that would not take hours, and if they did opt for that it would give him ample time to shift his ambush elsewhere.

He pulled the butt of the Winchester tight into his shoulder, and rested his left hand on the rocky edge of the ledge and laid the barrel between his thumb and forefinger. Dropping his head to look along the sights, he focused on the gap between the rocks where the first rider must appear.

If they were using both horses, he would let the first one pass, and hit the second. It would be natural for the first rider to pause and look back to see what had happened to the second, and the pause would give him time to shift his aim and fire a second time. The marksman in him, took over. He laid his aim where the body of a riding man would be, a couple of feet above and behind the saddle horn. He was a remarkably good shot and he knew he would not miss.

But he did.

The first rider came through the slot at an easy canter and, as the horse emerged from the gap, the rider clapped in his spurs and the mount went off like a bobcat with its tail on fire.

The second came through at a flat run, with the rider

laid low along its back, and hanging down the far side of its neck. The waiting sniper was taken by surprise at the speed of the targets, and had to shift his aim down a foot or so, during which time the running horse suddenly stopped.

The sniper, following through the expected run of the horse, fired a couple of feet ahead of it to allow for its travel, so his bullet hit the ground ahead of the animal, and whanged off into the heated air.

He jerked his aim back, just as the horse took off again in a series of bounds, and he missed it again, this time behind.

Swearing and thrown off balance, he half stood to swing the rifle, working the lever at the same time, and a bullet howled off the edge of his ledge and past his face. It made him flinch and the third shot went astray as well.

Time to go. He stood and ran back along the ledge and round the curve of the rocky tower. He had left his horse tethered to a lump of scraggy bear grass, and it was still there, unmoved by the crashing reports.

He ran down the side of the rock towards it and, as he did so, something moved in the very corner of his vision and instinctively, he dived for cover.

He was not quite quick enough. The first shot clipped the heel of his boot and slammed his foot sideways, so that he tripped himself and went sliding face down along the ledge. His rifle flipped out of his grasp and fell down the side of the rock, clattering uselessly away out of reach, and in his desperate attempt to regain it, he slid half on and half off the ledge, arm outstretched.

The second shot hit him in the back of his exposed shoulder, smashing his shoulder blade and paralysing his right arm.

The shoulder went numb, though he knew what had happened and realized that when the shock wore off, it would be agonizing. Worse, his right hand was his gun hand, and to get his pistol out he had to roll on his back and reach across his body with his left hand.

Lying on his back, he managed it and cocked the action. There was no following shot, so he realized that in falling flat on the ledge he had put himself out of sight of the shooter lower down. But to shoot, he would have to raise his body and extend his left arm.

Below him, he heard the sound of hoofs on the rock and knew that both his enemies were down there, now. Also, of course, the woman. A wave of rage rose in his throat. That interfering bitch! Because of her his perfectly good scheme to get Wells Fargo to carry his loot out of harm's way had gone disastrously wrong.

He raised his head slightly to peer down into the rocks, and saw a glimpse of her, as she slipped between two of the large boulders. If she moved, she would have to expose her body to his aim and if she did so, he could at least kill her.

The man they called the Mexican rolled on to his left shoulder and looked down at his right. The shirt sleeve was a mass of blood, and it left a huge splotch on the rocks where he was lying. His right arm was just a trailing useless encumbrance.

So what if he had lost his rifle? In this state it was useless to him anyway. He cocked the long-barrelled Colt and held it by his head as he wriggled himself into a shooting position. She was still there, behind her rock, but he saw a suggestion of movement by the edge of it.

She was preparing to make a dash – he was sure of it.

The only place she could dash to was another lump of rock some yards away, so she would be in the open and with her encumbering skirts and petticoats, slow-moving, for several seconds.

Time enough to aim and fire at least twice. Time enough to kill.

He steadied his wrist on the edge of the ledge, took a bead a yard to the left of the rock which sheltered his prey, and steadied his aim.

There! A dark mass erupted from the sheltering rock, and he fired instinctively, and saw it smashed sideways. Flicking the hammer back, he snapped off another shot even as the dark mass was falling, and saw it twitch. Two hits!

But the dark mass simply crumpled on to the rocks, flat as a collapsed balloon and, as he stared, dumbfounded, there was a glimmer of white flesh as the girl herself emerged from behind the rock and ran, bare legs flashing out, to the shelter of the next boulder. He fired again, belatedly, but his concentration had been on what he now realized must have been her empty dress. He fired late and he missed.

He stifled a sob of rage and eared back the hammer of the Colt again, preparing himself to jump from the ledge and run down on the girl. But his legs seemed strangely sluggish and all he managed was to hunch himself up on to his knees, useless right arm trailing and the Colt clutched with all his strength.

'Drop it!' said a voice with death in it from above and behind him, and he twisted his head to see that damned rancher standing on a rock near the ledge. He must have climbed up the side of the pinnacle out of sight while El

Mexicano was concentrating on the running horses, and now stood above him. There was no cover on the ledge, and the bandit knew he was not capable of the galvanic leap which would be needed to drop off the ledge into the broken ground below. He was trapped by his own ambush.

'Tom!' called the girl's voice from below. 'Are you all right?'

He looked down the hill and saw her, in her underwear, reaching for the ruins of her dress.

A chance! One last chance to hurt the people who had out manoeuvred him!

He grinned up at Bligh who, he realized, could not see the girl from where he was standing, and raised the gun for one last shot. It seemed unnaturally heavy, and a corner of his mind told him he had lost too much blood for this.

But one last shot – he had to take it.

He dropped his head to see along the sights. It was a long shot for a pistol and downhill, too, so he allowed for the drop. The trigger came back crisp and clean.

But as it fired, a hammer hit him in the back, and he was smashed down onto the ledge again. The pistol, too heavy to hold, clattered down the rock slope and jammed between two rocks.

It was the last thing he saw.

Chavez came up the slope cautiously and just missed seeing Frankie pull the bullet-holed dress back over her head. Because he was a Mexican and at heart a romantic, he found time to regret it, but also the faint touch of shame at the idea that he would take advantage of a young woman's embarrassment.

The regret, however, won out.

Tom Bligh came down the side of the rock pinnacle and examined the corpse. Chavez' bullet from below was the one which had crippled the outlaw, and Bligh's was the shot which had killed him. The bloodstained corpse, crumpled bonelessly on the ledge, looked somehow smaller than the man had looked in life.

His face had little to distinguish it from hundreds of others to be found in the mines and bars of Tombstone. He was quite wide across the cheekbones, and his eyes were deep sunken under his brows. There was a fringe of beard round his lower jaw, and his mouth was open, show-ing a strong set of healthy teeth.

'Like I said, he doesn't look Mexican, does he?' said the girl, leaning over to peer down into the dead face. 'Looks Anglo to me. I asked him about it, back in the cave and he just laughed. Didn't bother him one way or the other.'

Chavez said, 'He is Anglo. His name is Roger Bull and he comes from England, I think.' He shot a sidelong look at Bligh.

'There is a reward on his head in Mexico,' he said. 'A good reward.'

'And in Tombstone,' agreed Bligh. 'Which is closer. Will the Mexican authorities require a body?'

Chavez shrugged. 'Usually, of course. But it is a long way to the authorities in Mexico, and by the time I get it there, the corpse will not be recognizable. Perhaps a sworn affidavit from, say, Señor Earp will be enough.'

CHAPTER FIFTEEN

The reward was a good one, and covered a lot of the money Bligh had lost when El Mexicano stole the proceeds of the sale of his herd. Together, Bligh and the girl stood themselves the best dinner Tombstone had to offer at the Can Can restaurant, with champagne cooled in real ice shipped at a greater price than the wine itself.

Frankie, who was glowing in green silk cut low at the shoulders and tight at the waist, raised her glass to look at the bubbles in the wine, and took a long drink of it.

'It's OK but it ain't worth the price,' said Bligh, putting down his glass after a few sips. The bubbles went up his nose and he sneezed, which made Frankie laugh, which in turn made her hiccough. Bligh laughed at her in turn, and they found themselves giggling like schoolkids.

'What are you going to do with your half?' he asked her, when they stopped laughing, and her face instantly went sober and serious.

'My half?' she said.

'Well, sure. Any girl who cuddles a rattler for hours gets to earn some of the reward, I reckon,' he said, surprised. 'When she strips off to divert a bandit's attention, that clinches it in my book. Here.'

He put down on the table a leather pouch which chinked, and she opened it and peered in.

'Gold!' she said, doubly surprised. 'You're handing over gold!'

He grinned. 'Kind of looks pretty good, don't it?' he said. 'You earned it, girl, you take it .'

There was a short silence while she studied his face with wondering eyes.

'You know, Tom Bligh, you really are a good, honest man,' she said. 'I haven't met many along your lines. You're pretty thin on the ground in these parts.'

He was embarrassed, and it showed. For their dinner he had bought himself a new set of clothes, which included a white shirt and a bolo tie which chafed his neck. He put a finger into the collar and pulled it loose, while he fiddled with his coffee cup.

When she put her own bag on the table, he glanced at it, surprised. It was an unusually large one, and it thumped on to the cloth surprisingly heavily.

'What I want you to do now,' she said, 'is to open this bag and tell me what you see.'

Wondering, he opened it and tilted it to the light. Paper-wrapped cylinders half filled the bag. He took one out, wondering at its weight, and opened the end. Gold coins poured, clunking, on to the table. In the yellow light of the lamps in their little alcove, the coins glowed like a river of fire.

'But this is—' he started, then stopped as he considered the implications of her haul.

'That is the money he took off you on the coach,' she said quietly. 'It was in his box, and I stole it. He didn't find out at Dragoon Springs Station. So I brought it with me to

155

Tombstone. It's been in my room ever since.'

He sat staring at her for a long moment, then gave a surprised whoop of laughter.

'You had it all the time, you little wildcat,' he said. 'All that time we thought he was chasing you for nothing, the man was right: you did take his money!'

She had the grace to flush. On her it looked very pretty.

'He had no more right to it than anybody else,' she said defensively. 'It was loot. He took it off other people. I took it off him.'

'But you nearly died for it!'

'He would have killed me anyway as soon as he had his hands on it. He had a good try, even without the money. He was never quite certain I had got it. Just thought it was possible.'

'And how did you get it?' The implications of her confession were just dawning on him. This was his money, all right, but the rest of the bandit's loot belonged to a whole lot of other people just like Bligh. People who had worked for it, risked their lives and their health for it. Honest folk.

'I took it out of the strong box before it left Maricopa Springs,' she said calmly. 'I was in the office when they were arranging the driver and the new horses for the second run. They needed a new pair of horses to replace the ones he shot, and while they were out harnessing them, the box was on the floor behind the counter.

'It wasn't locked, and my valise was still in the office, so I just transferred the money. It was stolen, anyway, and I expected to be in Tombstone before the theft was discovered.'

He shook his head in wonder. 'But they must have

noticed the weight.'

'They were using some rocks for doorstops in the office. I put one of them in. Nobody noticed.'

Until the bandit stole a march on his partner and made his own attempt to recover his money. Another thought struck him.

'How did you know whose loot it was?' he said. 'You never saw him without his mask, did you?'

She shook her head and sipped at her champagne.

'I didn't recognize him. Like you say, I never saw him without his mask. But I did notice him recognize me. When he came in the office to leave his parcel for the strongbox, he did a double take, almost turned and ran.

'Now, I'm used to men taking a second look at me, but I'm not used to them running away. Usually the opposite. So it made me look at him over again and it set me thinking.'

He tossed back the remains of his champagne, grimaced and called the waiter for whiskey. It came with a beer chaser, and he drank from that first.

'So what are you going to do with the rest of it?'

She shrugged. For a moment, her hand stroked the heavy bag and then she sighed.

'I suppose it has to go back. At least I still get the reward money from you. That's more than I started out with. Just take me a little longer to get what I want, that's all. Pity, but as you say, this money was stolen, and it will have to go back.

'What do you think of the Earps?'

He sucked his teeth for a moment, then admitted, 'You'll hear a lot of talk about whether they are any more honest than any of the other galoots round here, but one

thing's for sure – they're the winning galoots. They repre-
sent the best chance at law and order we got right here
and right now.

'Chances are every tinhorn between here and Santa Fe
will claim he was robbed by El Mexicano, and half of them
will be telling something like the truth. Leave it to the
Earps to sort it out. That way nobody's shooting at you.'

She considered for a moment, then nodded.

'OK, Tom. You call the shots. You've done all right so
far. The horses will just have to wait.'

He glanced up, surprised. 'Horses?'

'I was planning to get myself a little horse ranch. I love
horses. Brought up with them, way back. So far I've been
lucky working in saloons. Luckier than I should have been
anyway.

'But sooner or later, that luck's going to run out. Some
gun-crazy drunk's going to blast off in the wrong direction, or some clumsy miner's going to think I'm dealing
them off the bottom of the stack, and the luck will run out.

'Sooner I'm out of the gambling business, the better.'

She was looking at him very directly over the rim of her
champagne glass when she said it, so he did not think for
a moment that the words were careless ones. The more he
thought about them, the fewer objections he could think
of. But he needed to think things out carefully.

'I reckon I better make for the sack,' he said. 'See you
for breakfast?'

'Could be,' she agreed and let him accompany her
upstairs to her room. There, she turned in the doorway,
leaned forward and kissed him lightly on the lips.

'Good night, sweet prince,' she said, and slowly closed
the door. He went down the corridor to his own room and

took off the bolo tie and his fancy vest. Then he looked at himself in the mirror, and swore at what he saw. A tall, broad shouldered man who knew more about cows than he did about women, and saw more of them, too.

He walked back down the corridor to her room and knocked. The door opened and she poked her head round it.

'Listen,' he said hesitantly, 'I was thinking. I got plenty of land, and no horses. Maybe. . . .'

She took him by the front of his shirt and hauled him round the door and into the dimly lit room. The green silk dress was lying across the bed and a pile of petticoats across the chair.

'Don't think,' she said. 'We'll do the thinking later, out on your spread. Tonight, just do.'

So he did.